The Wedding

THE OUTSIDER SERIES
BOOK SEVEN

LORHAINNE ECKHART

The Wedding Paperback Copyright © 2022 Lorhainne Ekelund
Editor: Talia Leduc

ISBN-13: 978-1998775354

Give feedback on the book at:
lorhainneeckhart@hotmail.com

Twitter: @LEckhart
Facebook: AuthorLorhainneEckhart

Printed in the U.S.A

The Outsider Series

The Forgotten Child (Brad and Emily)
A Baby And A Wedding
Fallen Hero (Andy, Jed, and Diana)
The Search
The Awakening (Andy and Laura)
Secrets (Jed and Diana)
Runaway (Andy and Laura)
Overdue
The Unexpected Storm (Neil and Candy)
The Wedding (Neil and Candy)

The Friessens: A New Beginning

The Deadline (Andy and Laura)
The Price to Love (Neil and Candy)
A Different Kind of Love (Brad and Emily)
A Vow of Love, A Friessen Family Christmas

The Friessens

The Reunion
The Bloodline (Andy & Laura)
The Promise (Diana & Jed)
The Business Plan (Neil & Candy)
The Decision (Brad & Emily)
First Love (Katy)
Family First
Leave the Light On
In the Moment
In the Family: A Friessen Family Christmas
In the Silence
In the Stars
In the Charm
Unexpected Consequences
It Was Always You
The First Time I Saw You
Welcome to My Arms
Welcome to Boston (A Paige & Morgan Short Story)
I'll Always Love You
Ground Rules
A Reason to Breathe
You Are My Everything
Anything For You
The Homecoming
When They Were Young (Link included FREE with The Homecoming)
Stay Away From My Daughter
The Bad Boy
A Place of Our Own
The Visitor
All About Devon

Long Past Dawn
How to Heal a Heart
Keep Me In Your Heart

The Friessen Family

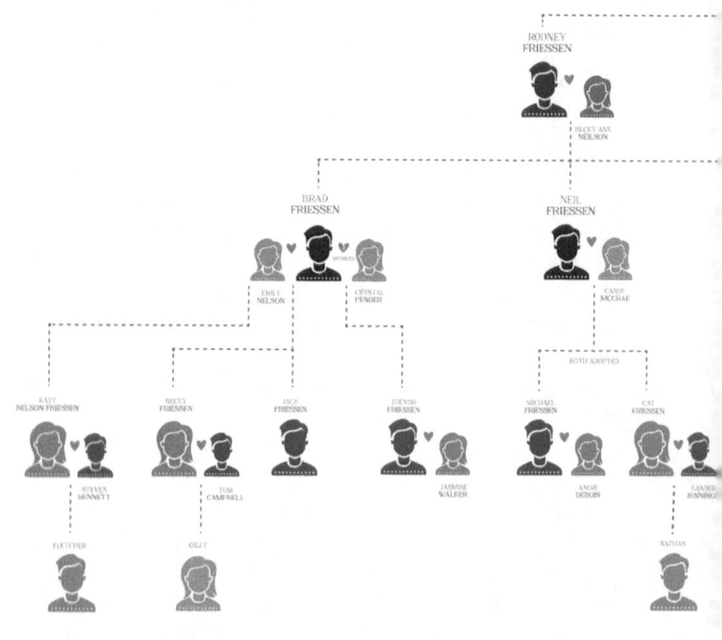

<table>
<tr><td>

The Outsider Series

THE FORGOTTEN CHILD	BRAD & EMILY
A BABY AND A WEDDING	BRAD & EMILY & *and Jed, Jed, Bradley & Becky*
FALLEN HERO	JED, DIANA & ANDY
THE SEARCH	JED, DIANA & ANDY
THE AWAKENING	ANDY & LAURA

</td><td>

The Outsider Series

SECRETS	DIANA & JED *with the entire Friessen Family*
RUNAWAY	ANDY & LAURA
OVERDUE	JED & DIANA
THE UNEXPECTED STORM	NEIL & CANDY
THE WEDDING	NEIL & CANDY *and the entire Friessen Family*

</td><td>

The Friessens:
A New Beginning

THE DEADLINE	ANDY & LAURA
THE PRICE TO LOVE	NEIL & CANDY
A DIFFERENT KIND OF LOVE	BRAD & EMILY
A VOW OF LOVE,	THE ENTIRE
A FRIESSEN FAMILY CHRISTMAS	FRIESSEN FAMILY

</td></tr>
</table>

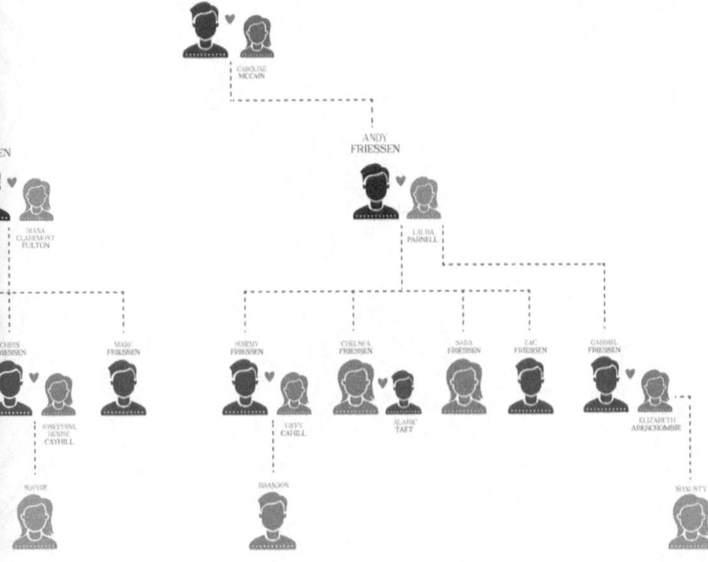

The Friessens

...HE ENTIRE FRIESSEN FAMILY	LEAVE THE LIGHT ON	KATY & STEVEN
...NDY & LAURA	IN THE MOMENT	BECKY & TOM
...ED & DIANA	IN THE FAMILY, A Friessen Family Christmas	THE ENTIRE FRIESSEN FAMILY
...EIL & CANDY	IN THE SILENCE	CAT & XANDER
...RAD & EMILY	IN THE STARS	DANNY & EVIE
...ATY & STEVEN	IN THE CHARM	CHRIS & J.D.
...ATY & STEVEN	UNEXPECTED CONSEQUENCES	CHRIS & J.D.

The Friessens

IT WAS ALWAYS YOU	KATY & STEVEN
THE FIRST TIME I SAW YOU	GABRIEL & ELIZABETH
WELCOME TO MY ARMS	CHELSEA & ALARIC
WELCOME TO BOSTON	PAIGE & MORGAN
I'LL ALWAYS LOVE YOU	JEREMY
GROUND RULES	JEREMY & TIFFY
A REASON TO BREATHE	TREVOR & JASMINE
YOU ARE MY EVERYTHING	MICHAEL & ANGIE
ANYTHING FOR YOU	
THE HOMECOMING	THE ENTIRE FRIESSEN FAMILY

—*"I love the alpha males and their ever strong headed wives. They love hard and strong but forever. Don't miss out on how Neil and Candy finally get their happily ever after."*

REVIEWER, JANET

—*"Loved the deep family bond she gave all the characters even when the plots took them to fighting they stuck together. Something we don't find often today."*

REVIEWER, PEBBLES

—*"Read the book-bittersweet but sometimes love has to go through fire to temper it and make it stronger."*

REVIEWER, AVTANNER

—*"It has heartbreak like you wouldn't believe but most importantly, love that will have you reading it over and over. I got this one the day after I first read Neil and Candy's story. It really is a beautiful book."*

REVIEWER, RAMONA

A man who's always planned everything, and a woman who's struggled alone—The Wedding will change their lives forever.

In THE WEDDING, Candy McCrae has everything she could ever want, and she's about to marry the one man she's always loved. He has money, he's powerful, he's drop-dead gorgeous, and he has a very close, attentive family with babies, nieces, and nephews running everywhere. For the first time, Candy has someone making decisions for her. So why is she so nervous?

Candy is the one woman Neil has always wanted, a woman who doesn't care about flash and glitter and status, and he can't get her to the altar fast enough. He has plans for his bride-to-be. He wants a family, lots of children, and for her to be a part of his world, with all its money, power, and million-dollar deals. He'll look after her so she'll never have to struggle again, and he's planned and organized everything.

She goes along with it until the wedding, when she takes Neil's hand to be his wife, and what she's refused to share will change their lives forever.

CHAPTER

One

"Wake up, sleepyhead." Neil slid his hand under the satiny sheet and over the inside of Candy McCrae's thigh. He was a rascal in the morning, and Candy was tired and could still feel the effects of being well loved the night before.

She rubbed her knuckles over her tired eyes and pressed into the corners, wiping the sleep away, then shoved her long, dark hair back. She hissed when he slid his hand higher and then pressed a kiss into her bare shoulder. "Neil, oh my God. I'm tired. What are you doing?" She gasped as his touch sent a jolt of pleasure through her.

He moved under the covers, touching her skin to skin, his hand skimming over her rounded cheeks and then across her flat stomach, up over her breasts. His touch was like a brand, saying to her without uttering one sound, "You're mine, my woman, and every part of you is mine alone to touch." She loved it! What woman wouldn't?

Candy tried to roll over to face Neil, but he stopped her with his body as he cupped her breast and pulled her against him. She slid her hand over the flexed muscles of his thighs, rubbing hair that was a mix of soft and masculine. He wouldn't let her turn to face him.

"Neil, I don't know if I can stand this. Let me touch you," she said, gasping when he nipped the back of her neck.

"Soon enough, but I mean to have you and taste every part of you," he murmured before running his tongue over her earlobe and nipping it with his teeth. Before she knew it, he'd rolled her over and draped her legs over his shoulder, sliding into her. The light from the morning sun highlighted gold flecks in the deep brown of his short hair, which was amazingly neat for a man who had spent most of the night inside Candy, doing all kinds of things to her that had her screaming out his name half a dozen times. It was a wonder she could still walk; the man was insatiable, and she stared into his brown eyes, which appeared to simmer the color of whiskey and burned into her as if he could read everything she tried to hide.

He held her head between his hands, pinning her down to have his way with her again. She couldn't move as he slid in and out, holding himself just above her, watching her, and she knew he could do anything to her and she'd let him. He loved it when she called out his name, and he'd wait until he knew she was nearly breaking apart before he'd tell her, "Say my name. Who do you belong to?"

She could never hold back. She couldn't stop herself as she screamed out, "Neil, oh my God, I'm yours!"

He filled what felt like every part of her, possessing her in a way that made her think she'd go mad, and in that same moment she knew that if he never touched her again, something inside her would slowly die.

After a moment, maybe two, they lay together; he was still inside her, his heartbeat matching the rhythm of hers and their breathing synchronized as one. She thought she heard voices outside, the sound of a car door slamming, but Neil didn't move. She ran her hands over his back, smoothing his tanned skin and taut, sculpted muscles with her fingertips. Still he didn't move, and she realized by his deep, relaxed breathing that he'd fallen asleep.

Candy glanced up at the window behind the bed and listened to the familiar voice of Maria, Neil's housekeeper, and two voices she'd never heard before. When Maria said, "How was your flight back, Señor Friessen, Señora?" Candy couldn't make out anything else, because she went into a full-blown panic. Neil's parents were here—now! A knot tightened in her stomach, a building anxiety, as she worried about what they would think of her. After all, she had nothing, and she wasn't sophisticated or worldly. Maybe they'd hate her, look down on her. She'd never said one word to Neil about her worries, because she knew he wouldn't have taken them seriously, but she couldn't help it. She stopped herself from waking Neil. Avoidance was sometimes a good thing. She decided she'd just hide out there and avoid them for as long as possible.

A loud, squeaky, braying and a crash as if something had shattered outside made Candy's blood turn to ice, and she shut her eyes. "Oh no, Ambrose," she muttered. Neil stirred, blinking just as a shout sounded below:

"What the hell is a donkey doing in my garden?"

The worst thing possible had just happened, and Candy widened her eyes in horror. She'd accomplished the one thing she had never wanted to do—start out on the wrong foot with Neil's mother.

Candy had managed to wiggle out from under Neil and throw on a skirt and tank top before racing out of the bedroom and outside, barefoot, only to see a wide-eyed Ambrose bolting with a bright red geranium sticking out of his mouth. Neil had shouted behind her to wait, but Candy hadn't listened as she raced down the orange concrete steps, taking in the horror and shocked expression on Neil's mother's face as the woman surveyed the yard. Even though the debris from the storm had been cleaned up—well, mostly—the lawn still bore the tire tracks from Neil's SUV, and for a moment, as she stared at Neil's mother, Candy couldn't help but feel responsible for the damage to the once immaculate grounds. This was ludicrous, she realized, except she couldn't make herself believe otherwise.

Stung by an overwhelming sense of insecurity, Candy reached out with shaky hands and grabbed Ambrose. As she lifted him, she sniffed an off scent, though whether it was her or Ambrose or both she wasn't sure. Her tangled hair drooped in her eyes, and it was then that it registered;

she had not one shred of underthings on under her clothes, which had been piled in a crumpled heap before she pulled them on—the same clothes Neil had peeled off her last night.

"Candy, what are you doing?" Neil yelled again as she held Ambrose. He was shirtless and barefoot, wearing just a pair of jeans, and he needed to shave. He looked like a wild man, which was so unlike him.

"Neil, I'm sorry he got into your mother's flowers. I'm so sorry, Missus Friessen. I'll move him," Candy said, stumbling. "He didn't mean any harm by what he was doing…." She wanted to find a hole and jump into it, and she just stopped talking as Neil's mother started to say something, staring at Candy as if she'd lost her mind before glancing over to Neil, obviously seeking help or an explanation. When Candy spotted Neil's father watching her in a way that had her face burning a nice, bright red, she really panicked. She began dragging and carrying Ambrose back toward the corral he had escaped from, out of sight, where she could somehow swallow her pride and gather back the dignity she'd lost in the mere seconds she's spent in front of Neil's parents.

NEIL WATCHED Candy as she dragged away that floppy-eared donkey, who behaved more like a rambunctious, untrained puppy than the barn animal he was. Candy was flustered and beautiful as she stammered, carrying on in a way he'd never seen before. No, he was seeing an insecure and vulnerable woman, a side of her he was positive she hadn't allowed anyone else to see. He had suspected it was buried somewhere underneath all of her little quirks, but she'd hid it well until he'd managed to peel away the thick layers that surrounded her. He also knew darn well that she'd gone off to hide from his parents for now.

His mother was staring at him, gesturing with her small hand to the garden, where Candy had disappeared. "That was Candy, your fiancée?" she said, stepping toward him in flat shoes, beige slacks, and a light green shirt. Her graying brown hair was cut in a short bob.

"That was Candy, yes."

"She seems a bit high strung there, son," his dad said as he came up behind him, patting his shoulder. "We obviously woke you two."

His mother gazed upward and shook her head. Neil didn't want to talk with either of his parents about what he'd been doing with Candy moments before they'd arrived, so he cleared his throat roughly and felt his face warm. Both Rodney and Becky exchanged an odd look, one that Neil didn't miss.

"Hey, so how's my nephew? Did Diana and Jed pick out a name for the big guy yet?" Neil said, crossing his arms as he realized he was bare chested. This modesty was so unlike him.

"Christopher Angus, after your grandfather," Becky said. Her gaze swept over Neil again in a puzzled sort of way, and she glanced in the direction Candy had scampered off to. "Maybe you should go after her, and after you two are, uh…" His mother cleared her throat and then lifted her chin before continuing. "We'll have lunch on the verandah. Go get dressed."

Neil's father raised his eyebrows, and there was a flicker of amusement in those light blue eyes. He followed his wife into the house, and Neil sighed before starting across the freshly clipped grass in the direction Candy had gone.

"Candy!" he called out, but she didn't answer.

Candy leaned against the concrete wall of the garage that backed onto the house, overlooking the rough corral that currently housed her horse, Sable. Ambrose toddled over to Sable and acted as if the commotion a moment ago hadn't happened. Candy stared at the corral, wondering how he had gotten out. Later, she would walk around the perimeter, but for now she was barely decent and had no intention of coming out of hiding any time soon. She knew she was being cowardly, and, as she wrapped her arms around her thin shirt, she hoped some wisdom or inspiration would suddenly fall from the sky. She prayed it would—something, anything to help her as she listened to Neil's shouts, which she had no intention of answering. She had no doubt he would just drag her back into the house to face his parents.

Neil Friessen was a hot, sexy, drop-dead gorgeous and confident man, the man she was going to marry, the man she had fallen for hard and fast. Oh, she realized now that she had always loved him, even when she thought she hated him. That had always been a big old lie, one she had told herself to protect her heart. Candy had learned the hard way that sometimes it was easier to pretend, and she still had a hard time understanding how Neil could love her when he could have any woman he wanted. She wasn't sophisticated, a polished debutante who could schmooze politicians and corporate billionaires. She didn't have soft, silky hands or long, painted fingernails. No, she had short, stubby nails, always with dirt under them, her hands were rough in spots, her face was tanned, and she burned her nose on a regular basis when she refused to wear a hat. Candy was used to hard, backbreaking work, and she would rather shovel out a barn than sit in some five-star establishment in a gown that cost more than she'd make in a lifetime, worrying the entire evening about spilling something on herself. Her clothes were modest, simple, and comfortable.

"Why didn't you answer me?" Neil said, appearing beside her. She hadn't heard him coming; she'd been so twisted up with worry and dread that she jumped.

"You scared me," she said, putting her hand over her rapidly beating heart. She wrapped her arms around her narrow waistline, feeling naked in her thin top and skirt.

Neil stepped closer and put both hands on her shoulders, sliding his palms down over her bare skin, holding her still. He put his fingers on her chin, tilting it up so she'd look at him and see the impatient, hard look he wore at times. She knew he wasn't about to be pushed around by anyone, even her—not that she was the manipulative type who would stoop to something like that. No, Neil Friessen had an inner strength. He liked to arrange, handle, and control. Candy had become intimately aware of how dynamic a force he was. He knew what he wanted, he had a clear vision, and he didn't let much stand in his way. She had lost everything in the storm, and he had even purchased brand-new clothes for her, picking the color and style of everything right down to her underwear. She'd have preferred to wear a pair of jeans that morning, but for some reason Neil liked her in a skirt.

Before Neil swooped in and rescued her when the storm pinned her down, she had handled everything: buying feed for her horse, bringing in the hay, maintaining the property her dad had left her, even trying to manage her lack of credit and bare-bones bank account. She had eventually lost her property to the bank, and Neil had taken over everything.

"Candy, aren't you listening to me?" Neil said, sounding somewhat annoyed. "What the hell are you doing, hiding back here? Come on. Let's go inside, get cleaned up. Mom and Dad want to meet you. We're going to have lunch together." He didn't give her time to answer, just took her arm and started leading her back to the house, but she dug her heels in and gripped his arms when panic started to lick the back of her throat.

"No, I'm not going back in there. I can't face your mother right now. What must she think of me? Did you see how she looked at me? She must think I'm an absolute idiot," Candy said, glancing over her shoulder and putting her hand on Neil's bare chest. She loved the feel of his pecs and abs, his magnificent body, the chest hair that trailed down, disappearing into the waistline of his jeans. She could stare at his body all day and never tire of it, and the man knew how to use it, too.

"Candy, you're being ridiculous. Stop freaking out. I can see the way you're retreating into yourself, and you need to stop it. Mom and Dad want to get to know you, and they're going to love you like I do. Just give Mom a chance. She was caught off guard. Ambrose surprised her, is all." He was so warm as he stepped to her, pulling her closer. She loved the way he surrounded her with his body and made her feel as if nothing could ever harm her. He touched her forehead and slid his thumb over her furrowed brow. "You're worrying about something. I can see it. Just trust me, okay? I'm not going to let anything happen to you. We're going inside, getting showered and dressed, and everything is going to be fine."

She didn't know how he had done it, but before she could speak, Neil was guiding her across the lawn. "Neil, did you see what Ambrose did? He didn't know any better," she said, feeling a bubble of laughter burst out. She slapped her hand over her mouth as she pictured Becky's face and Ambrose, wide-eyed, with her geraniums dangling from his mouth.

"That wasn't your fault, and that naughty problem child we have… well, I'll make sure I take care of the corral so he can't slip out again," Neil said, hugging her closer as they both stepped barefoot into the house and slipped quietly upstairs, back to his room.

Four

"Candy, have you put any thought into what kind of wedding you want?" Becky, Neil's mother, asked. She sat across from them at the round table, which was set with a white tablecloth, on the covered patio just off the main dining room.

They'd just been served a lush salad filled with fresh greens and topped with goats' cheese, and Neil watched as Candy picked at her dish. He didn't think she had put one bite in her mouth, and she kept sending nervous glances first to his mother and then his father. He could tell that everything he'd said upstairs to calm her down had done little to ease her anxiety, and he'd reached under the table and patted her leg a number of times to remind her. The last time, she knocked her knife to the ground.

"Oh, I'm so sorry," she said, scooting back her chair and bending over, scrambling to pick up the knife.

Neil's mother shot him a look across the table as if she was at a loss. Candy was wound so tightly, a ball of nerves, and there was little he could do at this point to calm her that wouldn't add to her acute embarrassment, so he took a breath and scraped his chair back, taking the knife from Candy when she went to set it back beside her plate. "Don't worry, honey. I'll get you another," he said, sliding her chair in.

She darted him a glance with smoldering brown eyes that pleaded with him not to leave her, and he could tell she was also fighting the urge to bolt, so he put a hand on her shoulder to steady her.

"Well, Candy, we want a big wedding, don't we?" he said. He'd been thinking about it for a while, and he wanted everyone from his business world, friends, family, and acquaintances to attend. He wanted witnesses to see how he had won over this beautiful woman and to announce to everyone what a lucky dog he was. She was his and his alone. He knew he was being possessive, but he didn't give a damn.

"Uh, I don't think we really talked about it," she said hesitantly.

Just then, Neil spotted Maria carrying a tray with their lunch, a fresh shrimp dish. He could smell the spicy aroma, so he breathed deeply. "Maria, could you bring out another knife for Candy when you get a moment?"

She rested the tray on the side table, and Neil set Candy's dirty knife beside it. "I'll get it for you right now," she said, starting to lift the plates before Neil stopped her.

"No, I can handle that, Maria." He tossed her an easy smile.

"Oh, you flirt, of course you can," she replied. She walked back into the house, and Neil scooped up the plates, noting the fresh salsa on the side, each dish full of white rice and plump shrimp. He set a plate in front of everyone, pushing aside Candy's salad. She stared at the dish and then glanced his way with a frown.

Neil sat back in his chair and watched as she picked up

her fork and started poking at the shrimp, and he noticed his father exchange a puzzled look with his mother's wide-eyed plea.

His mother leaned toward Candy. "Do you know that when I was going to marry your father, I had the worst attack of nerves?" she said. She smiled at Neil and then over at Candy.

"No, I didn't," Neil said, and he noticed Candy relaxing a bit. She no longer had a death grip on her fork. His father said not a word as he dug into his shrimp.

"I had met your father at school," Becky continued. "Your father and I went to Berkley at the same time. I was still living with my parents, who had a place in the Napa Valley. We weren't wealthy, but my father was a hard worker, and we weren't poor, either. I didn't understand the family your father came from until I met Angus, your grandfather. When Rodney took me back to the family ranch, he forgot to mention that Angus Friessen was as successful as he was; the president of the cattlemen's association and a senator! Well, I felt like a country bumpkin, way out of his league. I nearly called off the wedding."

Rodney stopped chewing and glanced over at Becky with a puzzled expression. "You never told me that," he said.

Becky reached over and patted his hand. "I didn't say too much, if you remember, when you took me home to meet your dad, but he sure had a lot to say to me."

Neil watched his parents and wondered why his mother was bringing this up. It was obvious she'd never mentioned it to his father from the dark look on his face, which was something Neil hadn't seen in a long time.

"What did my father say to you?" Rodney said, his deep voice holding a bit of an edge.

Neil glanced over at Candy, whose eyes widened. The

entire atmosphere at the table had changed, turning from one of a bride with a case of nerves to some underlying spark between his parents. Just what the hell was going on with them?

Becky pressed the cloth napkin to her lips. "Oh, he gave me a little warning, said I had better be a proper wife to you and that if I had some fancy idea of marrying you just for a comfortable life with an abundance of money, I'd best look elsewhere. The ranch would be left to you, Rodney, and would then go to the eldest son of the children we'd have, but it would never be in my name," Becky said. She set her napkin down, and Neil sat in silence as he watched his father hold his fork frozen in midair. A wave of emotions colored Rodney's face, and Neil wondered what his mother was trying to accomplish and how his dad would react.

Neil could hear Candy breathing beside him as if trying to go unnoticed, but she was failing miserably. Was there a problem between his parents? This was definitely not how they usually acted. Sure, they argued like any married couple, but they were an example of commitment and family and love. They were his role models. As he watched his mother again, he wondered why he'd never heard this story, and he could tell by the way she was sitting so still, watching his father, that she was deeply bothered by something that had happened so long ago.

"After all these years, Becky, you pick now to tell me that story? What's going on with you?" Rodney said in a tone that was a little harsh and so unlike him.

Neil glanced over at Candy. She didn't know where to look, and she took a bite of her rice and glanced at Neil as if expecting him to do something. Neil rubbed the stubble on his jaw and realized he hadn't shaved, but then, he'd had more important things to do with Candy in a hot shower.

"Mom, I'm surprised," he said. "That was a pretty rotten thing for Gramps to say to you. I thought you got along with him?" Neil hadn't met Angus Friessen, who had died before he was born, but he'd never heard his mother speak as if she had hard feelings.

"I never thought it was right, sharing it with you," Becky said, ignoring Neil and speaking to Rodney. "Your father hurt me when he said that. I didn't deserve to be treated that way. I wasn't a gold digger, and I also wasn't interested in creating a rift between you and your father. You had a tense relationship as it was, and then there was you and your brother, Todd." Becky tossed her napkin down.

Neil didn't miss the tension heating up between his parents. His mother was now glaring at his father. Maybe it was menopause, or was she past that? Rodney, though, just shook his head and dug into his lunch, taking another bite.

His mother let out a sigh. "So, Candy, tell me about the plans you have for your wedding."

Neil winced when Candy stilled beside him and glanced awkwardly at his mother, and he said, "A huge wedding," at the same time that Candy replied, "Something small." Neil blinked for a moment, taking in his mother's raised eyebrow and realizing that he and Candy needed to have a serious talk and get on the same page. Convincing her would be easy, though, he thought.

Five

Boy, was he mistaken. Convincing a woman that they had to have a huge wedding because it would leave everyone in ten counties talking for years about the wedding of the century, because it would be the right social setting for them, and because it would be in their best interest was going to be more of a challenge than Neil had expected.

The way she kept shaking her head, pacing his bedroom back and forth, about to wear a hole in the golden area rug at the foot of his four-poster bed, told him she wasn't convinced. She wouldn't look at him. In fact, she kept her mouth shut in a way that showed how stubborn she could be. But he knew that already. After all, he'd seen and experienced it, but he thought he'd softened it and pried it away. Well, at least that was what he did in bed. Maybe that was where he needed to convince her— on her back while he teased her and touched her until she begged and he could get her to agree to anything. That wouldn't be honest, though, and he hesitated a second as he stepped forward to touch her.

"I do *not* want a big wedding, Neil. I don't want to be on display for a bunch of strangers I don't give a crap about. This is personal, private. I would rather have no one, just you and me; have Francesco marry us—"

"Francesco!" Neil said, cutting her off. "Hell, no. We're having a priest marry us, in a church." Neil liked Francesco, but he didn't want just anyone marrying him; he wanted a marriage that was blessed and legal, and he somehow doubted that Francesco, who was a shaman, could legally perform a wedding.

Candy's arms tightened around her middle. She was pulling into herself again, away from him, winding herself up so tightly into her cocoon that it would take a lot of time and effort to ease her back out. "I want Franceso," she said. "I'm comfortable with him. I don't want some stuffy old priest who babbles all this religious dogma that I don't believe in, shoving it down my throat." She signaled with a wave of her hand that she was done listening to him.

The woman was testing him. That had to be it. What woman didn't want a church wedding?

"Candy, I want a wedding with you, a big wedding. Francesco is nice, but we're not getting married by a shaman. I want a real wedding," Neil said, realizing as soon as the words were out of his mouth that she was about to shut down and go to that place where her temper flared and her sound reasoning fled. He could see her tense as she fisted her hands and then glared at him. If he wasn't careful, she might slug him.

She opened her mouth to say something and started working her jaw. "You asshole, you sanctimonious prick. Are you kidding me? Getting married by a priest after you slept with me is a farce. I mean, really, what would a priest say if he knew what we've been doing in here? Oh, wait a second—you wouldn't tell him. It would be one of those little white lies of omission. Well, I'm not okay with that. Getting married by a priest does not make it a real wedding!" she snapped. This time, she threw both arms in the air, breathing hard.

"Okay, maybe we should just cool down," he said, reaching out for her arm, but she slapped his hand away.

"No!" She leaned in and then started to walk around him.

"Candy, stop," he said. He stepped behind her just as she reached the door and slid his arm around her waist, pulling her against him.

"Let me go," she pleaded. She pried at his arm and struggled as he pulled her closer, wrapping his other arm around her. He pressed his mouth against her cheek and then her temple, but he didn't let go.

He waited and kissed her cheek again, and she stopped fighting him. He could see how she had shut her eyes, and he slid his hand over the silky skin of her arm, running his lips lower until she offered her neck, leaning into him with a sigh. He took what he could, kissing her neck and tracing his tongue across her collar bone, reaching up and sliding the thin strap of her tank top over her soft, tanned shoulders as he nipped at the side of her neck. She relaxed into him further.

He knew he was being a bastard, but he knew how to strip her down, to make her pliable and knock down, once and for all, those walls she kept erecting between them. He turned her and pressed her against the door.

"Neil, you're a bastard," she began, but she didn't finish as he claimed her lips, sinking into the kiss deeply, tasting her, and she responded in a way that made Neil think his knees would go weak. She kissed him back with passion and ferocity, as if she'd been waiting for him for years, giving everything in the kiss. Neil couldn't think, as his good sense had been tossed out the moment Candy touched him. He had to have her now—he couldn't wait. This woman, with her touch, her body, could drive him half blind. He reached under her long skirt and slid down her underwear, lifting her and pressing his body into hers.

He reached between them and slid down his zipper, pushing inside her, and he froze, gazing into the heat and passion glowing in her eyes. She couldn't hide how she felt. She wrapped her legs around his waist, and her smoldering brown eyes turned their passion for one another into Fourth of July fireworks as he moved inside her.

"Oh, Neil," she said, breathless as she slid her hands over his cheeks, touching him, loving him.

"You will marry me. You are mine, by God…"

"Neil… oh, Neil, I love you."

He felt her come apart, and he couldn't hold back, shouting something right before he felt himself tumble over the edge into paradise, her arms clutched around his neck and every part of her tight around him.

He didn't know how long he held her against the door, but he slowly pressed his lips and forehead against hers. "Okay, change of plans. We're getting married, but not here. We'll compromise; just a family wedding at the family ranch."

He was still inside her when she let out a sigh and said, "Okay."

CHAPTER
Six

"We're going to have the wedding at the ranch, just family," Neil said to his parents as Candy leaned into his embrace. He glanced down at her, kissing the tip of her nose.

She couldn't believe that Neil had convinced her with this so-called compromise, and she was going along with it. She didn't know anything about the family ranch or his brothers, but every time Neil made love to her, he had this way of melting her resolve, organizing and arranging. She couldn't resist anything about him. The man was impossible and overbearing, but if he stepped out of her life, she didn't think she would be able to breathe without tearing a gigantic hole in her heart. So she agreed without understanding one bit of what she had agreed to, and here she was, attempting a pitiful smile while feeling as if she'd just been bulldozed.

"Just small, Neil, just family. Remember, you agreed. Not the three hundred people, acquaintances, and business associates you wanted. Something simple," she blurted out as her heart rate ramped up. She patted his chest and the crisp linen of his blue dress shirt. He was freshly shaven, his hair impeccably groomed, and for a moment, as she stood in his arms, she felt dowdy and way below his league. These were her insecurities, her fears of not being good enough, and she couldn't help but wonder at times, why her?

Becky and Rodney were seated in the comfortable living room, which was flooded by bright sun through the floor-to-ceiling glass doors. Becky set her book down, and Rodney folded the newspaper while slipping off his reading glasses.

"Have you talked to Brad?" Rodney asked.

"I think that's a great idea," Becky said before Rodney could finish. "Talk to Emily, but I'm sure she'd love it."

Candy squeezed his side. He glanced down and must have noticed her confused expression, because he said, "My brother Brad and his wife, Emily. You'll love her. I'll be calling him next to talk to him. How could it be a problem? It would probably be easier, with all the new babies, for Diana and Jed and for Andy and his twins. It's closer for them." He slid his hand down Candy's arm. "You know what? I'm going to call Brad now. No time like the present to get it planned." Neil started to walk away as alarm bells rang sharply in Candy's head.

She wondered if Becky had noticed, because she asked, "Well, when is the wedding?"

"Next week," Neil said as he strode out of the room. At this, Candy gasped out loud as all the air in her lungs left in a whoosh.

"COME SIT DOWN, Candy. You're looking a little pale. Rodney, why don't you go get some lemonade for us?"

Becky said as she somehow shooed Rodney out of the living room and seated Candy on the plump cushy sofa beside her. "Let me guess: You didn't know you were getting married this soon?"

Candy pressed her palms to cheeks that she could feel were becoming a little clammy. A week, seriously? What was the rush? She knew Neil wanted to marry soon, but she didn't realize he'd meant as early as next week. She felt the cushion dip beside her.

"Neil, I'm sure you've come to understand, doesn't sit around and wait for things to happen. He makes them happen," Becky stated in a clear, no-nonsense voice.

"Yes… but next week…" She was still trying to sort through her jumbled, confused feelings when Neil clapped his hands as he strode back in, all smiles.

"All set. Brad is thrilled, and Emily can't wait. In fact, they're helping to organize the wedding now: decorations, flowers—anything we need. Emily suggested having the service in the living room, since the weather is getting a little unstable, with lots of rain and maybe some snow, so an indoor wedding will be cozy."

Neil was beaming, and Candy couldn't believe how she just sat there as if the rug had been yanked out from under her. All she could think to say was, "I don't have a dress."

CHAPTER

Seven

Flying first class was something Candy had never expected to experience, not in this lifetime. She knew Neil was wealthy, that his family was wealthy, and realized she'd never understood the powerful circles they mingled in. Neil traveled first class, and she knew as well that the price of the airline ticket would be steep. Even flying economy was way out of her budget, but Neil didn't seem to blink at arranging, paying for, and handling everything. The stewardess smiled brightly and handed her a glass of champagne, and Candy just stared in confusion.

Neil cleared his throat and reached for the glass. "Ah, thank you. Candy, would you like some champagne?"

She stared at the bubbles in the glass flute and then reached for it. She'd never tried champagne, and of course she was curious, wondering what it would taste like as she accepted the flute from Neil. She couldn't smile, but she took a swallow and nearly choked, as it wasn't quite what she had expected. She grimaced and pulled a face.

"You don't like it?" Neil asked as he took a swallow from his own glass.

"How do people drink this stuff?" She didn't know why, but she took another swallow, the bubbles tickling her nose. Maybe it was the buzz she needed, courage or something, not that she ever drank much more than the occasional beer.

"Don't drink it if you don't want it," Neil said, taking the glass from her and handing it to the passing stewardess.

All Candy could do was stare as the stewardess walked away with her champagne. She squeezed her hand awkwardly.

"Buckle your seatbelt," Neil said. She fished around for it, and Neil reached across and buckled it for her before she could finish. He took her hand in his, linking their fingers. "You excited?" he said, smiling down at her. He finished his champagne, handing the empty glass to the stewardess.

She pasted a smile on her face. "Sure," she said, glancing out the small window beside her as the plane taxied down the runway and took off.

"It's going to be a long flight. Why don't you lean back and get some sleep?"

She didn't look over at Neil as she said, "Okay." She was rattled and confused by her feelings. She was self-conscious and felt like a fraud, sitting up in these wide leather seats. She gazed out the window as the plane steadily climbed, and then she shut her eyes.

NEIL COULDN'T HELP but be concerned about Candy. She was behaving rather oddly. He could feel her tension and knew she became quiet when she was uncomfortable. She'd been sleeping off and on, but she hadn't said more than a few words. Neil had occupied himself with his laptop, catching up on work and sifting through the dozen emails he'd received, particularly the one from redheaded Stella, his banker and friend, about Candy's property—the property he still hadn't told Candy he'd bought from the bank, paying off her debt so that the developer who'd tried to pick it up couldn't build all those condos up and down the white, sandy beach.

Yes, Neil still had his plans for that all-inclusive resort, but he also knew Candy would never forgive him if he went ahead and built it on her land; the land she believed she'd already lost to the bank. He glanced over at his dark-haired beauty. Her eyes were closed, her long hair draped over the curve of her breast. He noticed the goose bumps on her bare arms, then the short sleeves of her orange cotton T-shirt and her thin white skirt, and he frowned. She was going to be cold; fall in the Pacific Northwest wasn't warm. He wondered if she'd ever been to that part of the country. He'd never talked to her much about her childhood, and he realized there was a fair bit about Candy McCrae that he still had to learn.

He put a blanket across her and she stirred, opening her tired brown eyes and blinking up at him. "Sorry, honey, didn't mean to wake you. Go back to sleep."

She took a deep breath, but then she sat up and wiped at her eyes, the blanket slipping down. "How long did I sleep?"

"A few hours." He closed his laptop and tucked it in its case beside him on the floor. The leather seat rustled when Candy stretched. "Why don't you go back to sleep?" He slid his hand behind her neck and rubbed at the tightness, and she leaned into his touch.

"No, I'm only resting as it is. When do we land? Oh, that feels good."

"Soon. It's going to be a lot colder than you're used to."

She looked up at him with the oddest expression on her face. "I won't break, Neil. It may have been years, but I lived in Detroit before Dad bought that property on the ocean and moved us to Mexico. I'll be fine," she said, and he noticed the way her voice hitched when she mentioned her property. He needed to tell her, and he had meant to tell her long before now, except the time never seemed right.

"Candy…"

The captain came over the speaker and interrupted before he could finish, letting them know they were beginning their descent into Seattle and to fasten their seat belts.

"What is it, Neil?" Candy asked.

But something had him shaking his head and saying, "Nothing. Just can't wait for you to meet Brad and Emily and to show you where I grew up." He squeezed her hand, and this time she smiled back at him, some of her hesitation gone. Neil realized he'd once again missed his chance to tell her.

Eight

They landed a few hours later at the small airport terminal in Grays Harbour, Neil sitting beside the pilot in the small commuter plane they had transferred to from Seattle. The ride had been bumpy, and Candy was chilled even though her gray, cloak sweater had been overly warm in Mexico, but then, she did have bare legs under her thin skirt and bare feet in her sandals. She chewed on the inside of her cheek as she tried to think of what she might have packed that was warmer. Of all the new clothes Neil had bought her, there wasn't a single pair of jeans in the bundle. For some reason, he was obsessed with the idea of her wearing skirts. Maybe that was because they spent more time in bed than out, and he preferred the convenience of it. The fact was that Candy couldn't complain, because sex with Neil, on a scale of one to ten, was an eleven. Not that she had another man to compare it with, but she couldn't imagine that it could be better with anyone else, with the heights he took her to and the feelings he invoked in her, which drove her half wild.

In fact, just thinking about another man touching her had a chill climbing her spine.

"Are you okay?" Neil asked, sliding his arm around her and pulling her close. He made it so easy to lean on him, and for some reason she couldn't put her finger on, she felt some part of herself slipping away. But that was silly, so she forced a smile to her lips.

"Yeah, just cold. Should have worn jeans, but wait—I don't have any."

Neil didn't say a word, but the mischievous spark in his eyes said it all. "I'll get you a pair here. Suppose you'll need them."

"I think I do need them."

He leaned in to kiss her, and she felt so safe and protected in his arms, about to become lost in everything that was Neil. He had a way of possessing her, making her feel as if she were living and breathing.

"Hey, there you are!" a man with a deep voice called out. He was tall, wearing a brown cowboy hat, and he resembled Neil, although his face was a little rounder, his hair graying at the sides, and he wore faded jeans and a tan coat.

"Hey, big brother. Good timing—we just landed," Neil said with joy in his voice.

Candy watched as Brad gripped Neil's shoulder and slid his gaze down to Candy. He had the kindest eyes she'd ever seen, the same shade of whiskey-colored amber as Neil's, but they were softer, as if they'd seen more of life's hard side. She wondered what his story was.

Neil tightened his grip on her shoulder. "This is Candy."

Brad touched the brim of his hat. "It's a pleasure, Candy." He slapped Neil's shoulder. "So you're the woman who's had my dear brother here all tied up in knots, wondering if he was coming or going… for how many years, Neil?" Brad glanced at Neil with a familiar mischievous smirk.

"Hey!" Neil said, shoving at Brad.

Candy watched the playfulness between the brothers and sensed a bond that she wasn't familiar with. She realized she'd been longing for something like that, a family of her own. Neil was so rich in many ways, and she wondered if he knew how fortunate he was.

Candy found she was uncomfortable under Brad's scrutiny not just because he too was extremely handsome but because she hated being the focus of attention. She wondered about the other brother, Jed, and whether he, too, resembled these studs. What must Brad's wife be like? Was she stylish, wealthy, stuck up? Would she look down on Candy? She wasn't thinking—she was reacting. She knew her nerves were rather prickly right now, mostly from sitting on an airplane for hours, doing nothing. She never just sat around, ever, and her lower back was aching. Lately, though, Neil had done his best to keep her from doing anything too physical except when he had her in bed, which was maybe why she had been feeling a little bloated lately. She worried about whether she'd fit into her regular size five when she got a new pair of jeans.

"So when are Mom and Dad coming?" Brad asked as they followed him outside the small building to a shiny black pickup parked in the lot out front.

"Friday," Neil answered. "Mom said she didn't want to crowd Emily with the whole family showing up at once." He put his hand on Candy's hip and opened the back door of the truck, helping her in.

She was relieved, really, to be in the back, and maybe that was why she let out a sigh of relief.

Neil touched her hand. "Are you okay?" he asked,

studying her with such concern that she knew she'd never want for anything. Neil was so attentive, and he read her so well, but when he started to reach around her to buckle her seatbelt, she put her hand on his shoulder to stop him.

"Neil, I can fasten my own seatbelt. I'm not a child," she said.

He hovered for a second as his gaze slowly connected with hers. He frowned, and she felt him pull back a bit as if she had slapped him. Then she felt bad.

"Neil, I'm sorry. I'm just tired, I guess…" she began before stopping herself. What was she doing? This wasn't her fault, so why was she the one feeling bad?

"Candy, I know you can do your own seatbelt. I just want to take care of you."

She held his gaze for a minute before dropping hers, and he pulled away. She reached for her seatbelt and fastened it.

"Hey, Neil, is this it for luggage?" Brad called out, appearing behind Neil just as he shut her door. Candy shivered from the cool air, letting out another sigh.

The drive back to the family ranch—or rather, Brad's ranch—didn't take long. The men chatted, and Candy was thankful to have time to think and listen. She learned that Brad had three children—one of whom, his son, had autism—and that Emily was his second wife. He also said she was excited to meet Candy. Candy already knew Neil wanted children, as he'd told her over and over that he wanted a large family. Candy never said anything. She wasn't sure, now, as she thought about it, what she wanted. Being with Neil, everything had happened at warp speed. She could already be pregnant, she thought. She'd always been irregular, and just last week she'd had some light spotting. Maybe she should take one of those home pregnancy tests. She could get one here, maybe, but then she'd have to tell Neil, and that she didn't want to do.

Candy was amazed by the bare trees and heavy clouds, the grayness that turned this place and part of the world into something dark and depressing. Candy was used to sunshine and blue skies and warmth. Even the damp air, and, from the looks of it, the mud everywhere seemed so unlike Neil. Candy didn't mind, wondering if she'd be able to snag some boots and jeans from Emily and wander around the ranch.

Brad parked in front of a lovely two-story white home. It was older but appeared well cared for. A wheelbarrow was set beside the front steps. A petite woman with round cheeks and brown hair tied back in a ponytail smiled brightly when Neil climbed out, and he hugged her. She pulled back, and Brad slipped his arm around her, letting her snuggle against him. The top of her head reached his shoulder, and she was wearing faded blue jeans and a blue fleece jacket.

The woman looked around Neil to Candy's door, so she slid off her seatbelt and opened it, stepping out to meet another Friessen woman.

Neil didn't know what to make of Candy. He was still bothered that she had pushed him away when he tried to help her with her seat belt. What was going on with her? He could feel her pulling away and couldn't quite put his finger on why, but he also sensed that she was way out of her element here, and the only thing he wanted to do was make it easier for her. Of course he knew she could put her seatbelt on. He sighed. Maybe he needed to give her a little more space. It was just pre-wedding jitters, was all. Didn't all brides get a little off before the wedding?

"Neil, I'd like to meet Candy," Emily said, starting around him just as the back door popped open and Candy stepped out. She appeared pale, and he wanted to get her settled, maybe rest for a bit.

"Candy," Neil said, stepping toward her with his arm out. He recognized the tight smile she gave him as she stepped closer and allowed him to slip his arm around her. She fit so nicely against him, and he didn't want to let her go. "This is Emily, my sister-in-law, Brad's wife."

Emily reached forward to hug Candy, but at the last moment Candy held out her hand instead. It was awkward, but Emily accepted the handshake. "Pleasure to meet you, Candy. You must be tired and hungry from that long flight. Come on in, and let Neil and my husband bring in all the luggage," Emily said.

"Sure," Candy replied, glancing up at Neil and then pulling away, walking with Emily into the house. She didn't glance back at him, but he thought it was strange, the way she seemed to be isolating herself.

"Is everything all right, Neil?" Brad asked as he reached for the suitcases and lifted them from the back of the truck.

"Yeah, just a long flight. This is all new to Candy, being out here in this climate," Neil said as he grabbed a suitcase Brad had set down and reached for his computer bag in the front.

"I meant with you," Brad said.

Neil shut the door and studied his brother, who was watching him without his usual smile. "I'm fine. This is me we're talking about. When am I not fine?"

"Yeah, I know you. This is the woman who's had you twisted up for a long time, and now you've got her. All this seems a little rushed, you know?" Brad stepped closer.

Neil went to say something, but for a moment he was speechless. Didn't Brad get it, how long he'd wanted Candy? Brad would have done the same thing.

"Don't get mad," Brad said. "I can see you're jumping the gun, here. I just want to make sure you know what you're doing. I noticed some tension between you two. If you've forgotten, you two rode out a hurricane together, though I still can't believe you went in there to save her. Just make sure you know, when things settle after the adrenaline rush, surviving what you two did, that you're not making a mistake, rushing the wedding." Brad raised his hand to stop Neil from interrupting. "Just saying you should think about it. Sometimes it's best to take a few days to let things rest, think about whether you both want the same things. You run in some high-class circles, brother dear. Is she okay with that, supporting all them big projects you have on the go, schmoozing all those politicians you have on your side?"

"She'll do fine," Neil bit out. He wasn't about to admit that Candy wasn't comfortable in large groups, period. She preferred her donkey and horse to a group of snooty, high-society people. "Just drop it, would you? Candy and I are getting married on Saturday. We're starting a family. It's all good." Neil reached for one of the large suitcases. "So, which room are we staying in?"

"Emily has the guest room at the top of the stairs all ready for you," Brad said. He gave Neil another look and then started toward the house, carrying the other large suitcase. "Your old room."

Candy looked around the large country kitchen. It was green and white, large, square, practical, and nice. She loved the floor, worn, old hardwood, nothing fancy. It had been lived in, enjoyed. The living room they'd passed through was inviting and comfortable, with blankets over the back of the sofa, all in browns and golds, with western paintings on the wall and cream-colored curtains. There also weren't any useless knickknacks anywhere, and she appreciated that.

"Sit down. Can I get you some coffee?" Emily said. Candy had been thrown when Emily tried to hug her. She knew Emily was being nice, and she also knew she was being so prickly that she'd made Emily feel awkward. Candy hadn't expected to meet a casually dressed woman with dirt under her fingernails and mud on her boots. She had not a stitch of makeup on, and she looked great.

"Yes, I would love some," she replied. Her stomach growled, and she fought the urge to look away, embarrassed, because she was hungry as well. It was awkward, being here with Neil's family, people she didn't know. They were strangers.

Emily offered her a polite smile and poured her a cup of coffee. Then she turned to the fridge and took out a plate of sandwiches covered with plastic wrap, setting it on the table beside Candy before grabbing herself a mug. "Do you take anything in your coffee, Candy?" she asked hesitantly, and Candy felt bad. She was putting the woman on edge.

"No, black is fine. Thank you, Emily." She wrapped her hands around the hot mug and relaxed a little more when she noticed the chip in the side. The mismatched mugs were older, nothing fancy. She took a sip as Emily sat in a chair beside her.

Emily removed the plastic wrap from the plate. "I made these for lunch. Ham, and there's egg salad, too, if you don't like meat, that is."

Candy's mouth was watering. She loved a simple sandwich and couldn't remember the last time she'd had one. She picked up the egg salad with a bit of lettuce sticking out and took a bite. "Mm, this is good. Thank you."

Emily also took a sandwich half. The door banged shut, and the men's voices and footsteps stirred up a ruckus. Emily glanced at the doorway, but Candy didn't turn around, listening as they climbed the stairs until she couldn't hear them anymore.

"I hope they don't wake little Becky," Emily said, putting her elbow on the table and shoving a corner of the ham sandwich in her mouth.

For a minute, Candy blanked and wondered who little Becky was. Maybe her confusion showed on her face, as Emily gestured to the door. "My daughter. She's in preschool. Just turned four, but she was so tired, and I know that when she sees her uncle Neil she'll be over the moon and want to play with him." Just then, a little girl squawked upstairs. "Ah, there we go."

Emily didn't get up, and they listened to footsteps upstairs and Neil's laughter as the little girl squealed. Emily laughed and put her palm on the table. "Neil loves kids," she said, watching Candy closely. "You two planning on having any?"

"Neil wants a big family, lots of kids, he said. I've just never seen him around them," Candy replied, feeling anxiety build up inside her as she finished off her sandwich, looking down at the table and away from Emily's shrewd gaze.

"Are you all right?" Emily asked, reaching over to touch Candy's hand.

"Emily, I don't really know you, but could you help me get one of those home pregnancy tests?" Candy asked, instantly regretting her question because of the grin on Emily's face.

"Are you pregnant?" she whispered just as the men clambered down the stairs.

She glanced over her shoulder, worried that Neil might have heard. It would be even worse if Emily blurted it out, but when she looked back, she knew by the smile Emily had fixed on her face and the reassuring pat on her hand that she was keeping the secret.

"I'll get one for you," Emily whispered. She glanced up when Neil raced in with a brown-haired, little girl, squealing, tossed over his shoulder.

CHAPTER
Eleven

"You didn't eat much at dinner," Neil said as he helped Candy unpack their suitcases, putting clothes in the drawers and hanging the rest in the small closet Emily had cleared out for them.

"I wasn't that hungry. I had a sandwich earlier, and, I mean, it's not as if I did much to work up an appetite. We sat on a plane all day." She smoothed one of his dress shirts on a hanger and buttoned the top button. Even just touching the rich material, she could feel the high quality, and that made her uneasy.

She did, though, kind of like this small bedroom, with its comfortable double bed, a patchwork quilt, a chair by the door, and an older six-drawer dresser. The window overlooked the pasture, and, even in the dim light, she could make out the cows grazing and moving in the field through the parted gossamer curtain.

Neil put the empty suitcases under the bed and then patted the mattress. "Did you know this used to be my bedroom, growing up?"

Candy felt a flutter inside as Neil grinned and leaned

back on the bed. The top button of his dark blue dress shirt was undone, and he wore neatly pressed jeans. How did he manage to look so good all the time? She couldn't help herself as she walked toward him and put her hand in his, letting him draw her down beside him on the bed. She lay on her back, and Neil leaned over her.

"Are you okay, honey? You never really answered me before." He slid his hand over her cheek, smoothing her long, dark hair back. The way he looked at her, with such heat in his eyes, she prayed it would never fade.

A knock on the door stopped her before she could say anything.

Neil didn't move or let her up when he glanced at the door and said, "Come in."

Emily poked her head in, grinning at the two of them. "I hope I didn't interrupt. I was just running in to town. I have to pick up some things. Brad's getting the kids ready for bed. Candy, do you want to come with me?"

Neil glanced at her. "Well, you know, Candy, we could help Brad put the kids to bed. You could spend some time with my nieces and nephew."

He had the biggest grin on his face when he talked about the kids. Candy had nothing against them, any of them, but she also didn't feel the urge to jump in and look after any kids. Hell, no. She wanted to go with Emily, get out of the house. She also knew why Emily was asking.

"You know what? I could use some fresh air, and I'd love to go with Emily. Let me get my coat." She slid off the bed, her hand still in Neil's, and he frowned as if trying to read her and finding himself unable to do so. Well, she hoped he couldn't read her, anyway; so she bent down and pressed a chaste kiss to his lips before pulling away.

Emily stepped away from the door and glanced down

the hall, keeping her expression guarded. She said to Neil, "Brad has all the kids in the big bathtub in our bathroom."

Neil put his hand on Candy's lower back. "Are you sure you don't want to stay and help?"

She wondered why he was pushing it. Maybe he wanted to see how she was with kids. Was he testing her? He seemed so into them. She knew he wanted kids, she just hadn't realized how much. He would be an amazing father, but she was scared out of her mind at the thought of being a mother, because she didn't think she could be anywhere near as good with kids as he was.

"No, you go have fun. I'm going with Emily. I need to pick up some things, anyway," she said. Then she realized she didn't have a dime on her. How was she going to buy a pregnancy test with no money? Neil paid for everything—she had nothing—no property, not a dime to her name. She felt her face flush with embarrassment. She couldn't ask Emily to buy it for her.

"Well, what do you need? I'll get it for you," Neil said. He was yanking out his wallet, and she couldn't believe the wad of cash he had in there. He pulled out several bills and glanced from Emily to Candy.

"Candy, I'll wait for you downstairs." Emily touched her arm and then moved away.

Candy stared at the money and felt such loathing at herself for needing it and for being so dependent on Neil. She blinked back a burning in her eyes. What the hell was the matter with her? She wasn't weak.

"Hey, what's wrong?" Neil asked as he touched the side of her head so softly, gently.

When she looked up at him, she could see the depth of how much he cared, and it hurt, and it terrified her. Just days and weeks before, she had wanted this so much. "Neil, I don't have any money, and I feel like a nobody next to you. You have all this money. You just open your wallet and take it out, and you toss it away. I can't do that, and I don't want to take it," she whispered. She didn't want Brad or Emily to hear how pathetic she sounded.

He held her face between his hands. "Hey, you listen to me. I will always take care of you. You'll want for nothing. You take this, and you get what you need. I need to take care of you, so let me," he said. He touched his forehead to hers and held her to him before kissing her again. This time, she took the bills he folded in her hand and stepped away.

"Thank you, Neil," she said. She started down the stairs, but he stopped her.

"What do you need to get?" he asked.

She swallowed and stared back. She couldn't lie to him, but she also couldn't bring herself to tell him she needed a pregnancy test. At the same time, she didn't know why she couldn't say anything.

He must have suspected, as he inclined his head and gave her a look as if he knew she was hiding something. "Candy…" he said, starting down the stairs.

She looked down and back up at him. "I need a pregnancy test," she said.

CHAPTER

Twelve

Not only did Emily not take her to the store, but Neil had taken the truck keys and said he was driving Candy there himself. Emily appeared spooked for a minute until Candy filled her in on having told Neil about the pregnancy test, and Emily had slid her coat off, offered Candy a sympathetic smile, patted her arm, and said, "You're marrying a Friessen man, honey. You better get used to how they step in and take over everything." She'd then walked away, calling out to Brad as she went up the stairs.

The small drug store in Hoquiam was open late, and the shelf contained a dozen different brands of pregnancy tests alone. "What's with all the different tests? Geez, and look at the prices," Candy said.

"Stop worrying about the price, will you?" Neil said as he grabbed one box after another from the shelf. Holding six in his hand, he turned the pink one over and started reading. "So why didn't you want to tell me?" he asked, flicking her a difficult gaze.

"Tell you what?" she said. For a moment, she had

blanked, and he frowned. She realized he meant being pregnant. "Oh, I don't know. I…" She lowered her gaze, and he immediately put a finger under her chin and lifted it so she had no choice but to look at him.

"Come on, Candy. This is me. Don't hide anything from me. You should be able to tell me anything," he said. Neil had these tiny lines around the edges of his eyes, and they added to his mystery, making a man who was far too good looking even more so.

"I don't even know if I am. I've never been regular. I just feel…" She stopped, and he didn't interrupt, but she could tell he was listening with everything he had. "I don't want to disappoint you, and I sometimes feel as if this is too much. You want kids so badly, and I'm terrified. I saw how you are with your brother's kids, and I can't do that. I can't just step in and be like you are with them. Something must be wrong with me," she said. She wondered whether he'd walk away, now that she'd said it.

Instead, he allowed a slow smile to spread across his tanned face. "You could never disappoint me, Candy. Give yourself a break, too. It'll be different with our kids. You're going to be a wonderful mother. I know it." He held up the handful of pregnancy tests and said, "Well, let's go pay for these and give them a try."

"Neil, I don't think we need six. You're wasting money. One will do," she said, still reeling from what he'd said. She didn't share his confidence and could feel an overwhelming panic choking her as he led her up to the cash register and the overweight young man who was sorting scratch and win lottery tickets.

He set all six boxes on the counter. "Who knows which one's the best? Besides, it won't hurt to use them all," he said.

The guy behind the counter didn't look at their faces

as he rang up the amount and gave Neil the total. Candy reached in her purse for the money Neil had given her, but he shook his head and tossed some bills on the counter. He took the bag and her hand and led her out into the cold, damp night, where he helped her inside the truck.

NEIL WAS ENJOYING BEING BACK in this part of the country. As he drove the darkened highway back to Brad's with a very quiet Candy beside him, he noticed how tense she was. "Candy, are you worried about being pregnant? I know we haven't talked about this, but I thought you wanted kids."

She turned her head toward the window, touched her lip with her fingers, and then faced him. "I don't understand how I'm feeling. I love you, but I'm afraid that you're going to wake up and realize I'm not cut out for your world and that you made a mistake. I don't know how I'm going to be with kids. I thought I wanted them, but I'm scared. What if I'm a horrible mother?"

He reached his hand across the seat and linked it with hers. "You're going to be fine. Why don't we take it one step at a time? You get to pee on a stick first, find out if you're pregnant, and then let's just enjoy this time. Candy, would you stop putting yourself down? You're who I want."

She didn't let go of his hand, but he had a feeling, when she looked away again, that she didn't quite believe him. It had to be the hormones. He knew quite well, with his brothers, how Emily and Diana had been when they were pregnant. He would support Candy, waiting on her, pampering her while she grew large with his child, and she'd know how much he loved her. She was going to be an amazing mother.

It didn't take long to get back to Brad's. Neil held Candy's door open and helped her down. The bag in his hand, he walked her up the steps and opened the door for her. Brad and Emily were sitting in the living room when Neil shut the door. Emily glanced up from where she sat beside Brad, snuggled on the couch.

"Hey, you two," Brad said, keeping his arm around Emily when she tried to scoot off from where he was cuddling her. He wore a big grin as he glanced at the plastic bag Neil carried.

Candy toed off her sandals and stood in her bare feet. Neil realized he needed to get her some warmer clothes. Tomorrow, he'd take her shopping, maybe drive up the peninsula, take her into Olympia for the day. Neil handed Candy the bag, and she snatched it. He didn't miss the hint of color climbing her cheeks.

"Be up in a minute, honey," he said, watching as she hurried up the steps and noticing how quiet she was.

"So…" Emily started to say, her blue eyes flashing with a teasing spark.

"So nothing," Neil said. "We just picked up a few pregnancy tests. We'll see. Guess it's good that the wedding is this weekend. So, tell me, what about the minister? Is he booked? I guess I need to get a hold of the caterers, flowers, a band…"

Brad cut Neil off as he walked to the easy chair across from them. "Whoa, boy. How many people do you think are coming? When we talked on the phone, you said just family."

Emily patted Brad's shoulder. "You know this is your brother's wedding, and Candy's. It should be nice. Just remember, Neil, this house is only so big, and this time of year, with the weather… it's hard to plan something outdoors," she said, sliding her legs around. "I called the minister. He's booked in. There's a caterer, a local lady. She's really good, and you and Candy can talk to her tomorrow. For the flowers, you two just need to pick colors. Brad already has someone in Olympia coming out to decorate and set everything up in the house. It'll be in the living room, and we'll set up a buffet in the dining room. Oh, and did Candy get a dress?" Emily asked.

"No, she didn't. We'll take care of it tomorrow when I take her shopping. Olympia has some wedding stores, right?" Neil asked.

Emily slipped out of Brad's arms and wandered into his office. She returned a few minutes later with a card and handed it to Neil. "Call this lady, Veronica Tanner. She's a wedding consultant, and she'll handle everything you need. When I spoke with her, she was a little freaked out when I mentioned a wedding this weekend, but she's flexible, and she said it would be possible to pull it off if it's small. She can put you in touch with designers, too, and someone to make your wedding cake."

Neil looked at the pink and white card with the name of the wedding consultant and decided to let her handle everything, just like a good secretary would. "I'll call her in the morning," he said. He stuck the card in his shirt pocket and then glanced up the stairs. "I'm going to head up, see what my fiancée is doing. I'll see you two in the morning."

They said goodnight, and Neil hurried upstairs. The bathroom door was open, and the light was off. He pushed open the bedroom door to see Candy perched on the edge of the bed, the pregnancy tests scattered beside her, still wearing her gray sweater.

"Did you take one?" He gestured to the boxes beside her.

She nodded. "Yeah," she said, pointing to the dresser across the room. "Just waiting, but it also said it's best to do it in the morning and wait two minutes for the results."

She was gripping the mattress, and she had a look in her eyes that he hadn't seen before. He wondered for a moment, by the way her face had tightened, if she was scared. "Has it been two minutes?" he asked, staring toward the dresser. The bed squeaked behind him.

"Yes," she said. He turned to face her as he picked up the stick, and she was squeezing her hands together. "What does it say?" Her voice sounded dry and very scared.

He glanced at the stick, but he was at a loss. He'd never seen a pregnancy test before, as he'd never put himself in a position for an unplanned pregnancy. He used protection and made sure the ladies he was bedding also used it, except with Candy—because he wanted her pregnant. "What's it supposed to say?" he asked.

She let out a sigh that sounded a lot like relief. "There's supposed to be a plus sign in the center of the stick if I'm pregnant."

"You mean like this?" he asked, holding up the stick with the bright pink plus sign, and he watched Candy's eyes widen as she slapped her hand over her gasp.

Thirteen

What a week it had been. Candy was in the kitchen, helping Emily clean up after dinner. They were expecting Jed and Diana and their two children, little Danny and the new baby, though for the life of her Candy couldn't remember what the baby's name was.

"So how are you feeling?" Emily asked, wiping down a spot on the counter.

If there was one thing Candy was tired of, it was everyone's excitement over the baby she was carrying. Being pregnant was supposed to be the happiest time of her life, but she'd been in a state of shock since Neil had showed her the positive result on the stick four nights ago. She'd spent the next few days being dragged around by Neil to Olympia for shopping, meeting with a wedding coordinator, and being fitted for a wedding gown she hadn't even picked out. Neil handled everything, including the sexy, long, white wedding dress that showed a generous amount of cleavage, with a low-cut back and satiny material that flowed in a mini train. The dress was stunning, and she felt like a princess, one that was on a glass pedestal, being showcased to everyone in a way she absolutely hated. She'd said nothing.

When Neil ordered a five-tiered cake, she stared at him as if he'd lost his mind. Who did he think he was feeding? The caterer had come up with so many dishes, hors d'oeuvres, and fancy things to eat, some that she'd never heard of. There were mountains of flowers, and the music—good Lord, Neil had hired a local string group. He had even suggested that Emily stand up for Candy, and Diana, too, even though she'd never met her. Candy had said nothing and just let Neil handle it all. It was supposed to be a small wedding, but Neil had a weird idea of what a small family wedding was. This was posh, fancy, expensive, and she was terrified. She couldn't help but feel as if Neil were molding her into something she wasn't.

Hell, she hadn't even met Neil's other brother Jed. Then there was his cousin, Andy, and his wife, who were coming as well. There were also a few local neighbors the Friessens had known forever, but there was no one for Candy.

"Candy, are you okay?" Emily asked. She leaned closer and touched her arm.

Candy fought the urge to cry, because Emily had been nothing but kind. She was a wonderful mother for her autistic son, who didn't appear all that odd to Candy. "Emily, how do you do all this?" she asked as she set the dirty plates in the sink to be rinsed.

"Do what?" Emily asked, watching Candy with an amazing pair of blue eyes.

"You're so calm, yet you have three kids, and your eldest has autism. He looks good, but how do you do this, handle all this?" She wondered if her voice had caught, and she looked away. Maybe she shouldn't have said anything about Trevor.

"Trevor is actually from Brad's first marriage," Emily said. "It's an unusual story. I was married before, too, and Katie is from my first. When I set out on my own, Brad hired me to look after Trevor and the house. That was how we met."

Candy couldn't have been more shocked if Emily had said she'd recently gone to the moon. Maybe something in her expression said that, as Emily shrugged awkwardly.

"It is what it is, Candy. We fell in love, but it wasn't an easy road. I figured out Trevor had autism, and the hardest thing was telling Brad. Oh, he was devastated, but eventually he got him diagnosed and started therapy. He's doing so good now. You should have seen him before. He couldn't do anything, would scream and carry on. I couldn't take him out because I didn't know what he'd do. He'd jump on people who came to the house, he'd write on the walls... It was awful, but look at him now." Emily glanced over her shoulder at Trevor, who slipped into the kitchen, carrying his empty dessert plate.

He set it on the counter beside Emily and glanced up at Candy. "Do you like Lego Star Wars?" he asked.

Candy was at a loss. Maybe Emily noticed, as she said to Trevor, "Not many people know video games, and since when are we talking about video games? I thought you were helping your dad."

"But, Mom, I want to play Lego Star Wars. Please?" he added with a bright smile, through Candy noticed he didn't seem too interested in waiting for her response.

"No. Go help your dad and Uncle Neil," Emily said. Candy couldn't help watching the boy, who didn't realize she'd never figured out how to untwist her tongue and respond to him.

He walked away and said, "Okay, Mom." He sounded so happy.

Emily didn't say anything, and Candy started to feel bad, because she was pretty sure Neil would have been all over him, talking to him and chatting up a storm. Candy had just heard the word "autism," and her head was full of expectations for his behavior. She actually really liked the kid.

"I'm sorry. I should have said something to him. I hope you don't think…" She stopped talking when Emily shrugged.

"It's okay, Candy. Not everyone is comfortable around autistic children. He gets stuck on videos and TV, and for some reason talking about that comes so easily for him. The real work is having conversations about everyday stuff, in-the-moment stuff. We hope to get there one day, hopefully soon, but at least he doesn't have behavioral problems. He's doing really good. I mean, he used to be a handful, but now he's just a lot of fun. He still has a long way to go," Emily said, and it sounded as if she was rambling on.

"Emily, it's not the autism—it's children. I don't have a clue what to say to any of them. I'm nervous. What kind of mother am I going to be to this one? I'm terrified of all your children," she admitted, and her voice squeaked. She pressed a shaky hand to her lips.

"Oh, I see." Emily stifled a soft laugh and then rubbed her arm, glancing over her shoulder, maybe to make sure they were still alone. Echoes and laughter from the other room carried into the kitchen. The kids, Neil and Brad, whatever they were doing, were having a lot of fun. "Candy, give yourself a break. You're getting married on Saturday, in two days. Tomorrow the entire family is going to invade us, but don't worry. They're wonderful. You've just found out you're pregnant! Honey, you've got a lot on your plate, and you know what? There have been days I'm terrified of my children. Well, not really, but there isn't a parent out there who hasn't been scared to death around children, especially other people's."

Candy forced herself to nod, because she couldn't clear her throat to get a word out, but it still didn't make her feel any better. She wasn't natural at this, and Neil was. That was all there was to it. She was starting to feel a little shaky.

"Candy, are you feeling okay, really? You look a little pale," Emily asked again.

The fact was that she didn't feel great, not really. The smell in the kitchen had an odor that should have been pleasant but carried a sharp tang that was bringing a dull ache in her head.

"I think I need some fresh air. Do you think Brad would mind if I went out to the barn? I'd love to see the horses." Candy had been dying to spend time with the horses since she had gotten there, instead of being dragged around to store after store. She hadn't so much as touched a horse since leaving her Azteca gelding, Sable, at Neil's. She needed to touch a horse every day, because they kept her honest, grounded. She also wondered, though, being the basket case she currently was, whether being around a horse might not be the best idea.

"The horses aren't in the barn," Emily said. "Brad rarely brings them in, only if one of them is hurt or something. He doesn't believe in caging them into stalls like that. He's got five acres fenced off in the north field at the tree line where the horses are, behind the barn. It's too dark now, but why don't we go out first thing in the morning? I'm sure Brad will be fine with that."

Candy nodded. "Do you mind if I go lie down? I'm feeling kind of tired."

"No, you go," Emily said, rubbing her back, and Candy strode around the corner and stopped, watching Neil play horsey with two of the kids.

CHAPTER
Fourteen

"Hey, big brother. Where're Emily and Candy?" Neil asked as he met Brad in the kitchen, pouring a coffee.

"Emily took Candy out to see the horses, said they'll be back before breakfast." Brad gestured to the mugs. "We're supposed to listen for the kids, too, since they're still asleep."

Neil glanced toward the back door and the empty table where Emily would generally have laid out breakfast by now. When he had climbed into the shower, wanting Candy to join him, she'd still been in bed and said no, and when he came back to the room, dressed, she had already made the bed and left.

"Everything all right?" Brad asked, giving Neil a shrewd and questioning look.

"Yeah. I think I'll go see where the girls are," Neil said. He slipped his leather coat on and opened the back door. One of the kids was giggling from the top of the stairs, and Neil pointed. "Kids are up. I'll see you later for breakfast."

He stepped outside into the fresh morning and started

toward the barn. One of the ranch hands, in a ratty, beige cowboy hat, worn blue jeans, and cowboy boots, carried a hay bale from the barn and set it on the flatbed attached to the old rusty tractor.

"Can't believe that thing still runs," Neil said as the cowboy wiped his forehead and laughed.

"Oh, barely. Brad's got it held together with duct tape and twine, now," the cowboy said as he headed back into the barn.

Neil remembered that tractor. He was ten the first time he had driven it, and it had already been a part of this ranch for more than forty years then. "Hey, listen, you seen Emily and Candy?" he called out to the cowboy when he came out of the barn, carrying another bale of hay.

"Yeah, I think they're taking one of the horses out. Emily's got a thing for the new Paint. I told them to be careful, as it's been spooking lately."

Neil could smell the pungent aroma of manure, the dampness of the morning, but at that moment he had a chill and an unsettling feeling. Candy wouldn't climb on a horse now, would she, carrying his child? Dammit! He started at a jog behind the barn to the treeline, where Brad kept the horses. The gate was closed, and he ran faster.

He couldn't see them, and even after he had opened the gate and started inside, he had to really look. He spotted the horses gathered around a big feeder filled with hay, and he heard Emily leading the Paint down the trail. Candy was on its back. He started toward her.

"Hey there, Neil. I was just showing Candy the horses," Emily said, all smiles until she saw Neil's face. He was dark and angry, and he couldn't hide it. Emily appeared nervous and glanced up at Candy, who was holding on to the black mane of the tan and white Paint. Neil stopped just before them and waited before reaching out to take the lead from Emily. She stepped away.

"Get off, now!" he said. The horse tried to move, but Neil set his hand on its neck and then reached up, wrapping his arm around Candy's waist and setting her on the ground.

"Neil, what are you doing?" she snapped, slapping at his hand. The sparks shooting from her eyes cooled a bit when he stepped closer to her. He grabbed her arm and pulled her away from the horse. "Neil, stop it!"

He didn't let go. In fact, with one hand, he released the horse from its halter. "Let's go," he said. He held on to her, and he was so mad he was tempted to shake her. When she tried to pull away, he tossed her over his shoulder and put his hand on her bottom to stop her from wiggling. He glanced at Emily, who was watching with wide eyes.

"Emily, Candy is pregnant. I don't know what nonsense would go through both of your heads about getting on a horse, especially one who, from what I understand, spooks and is unpredictable."

Emily opened her mouth to say something and then closed it.

"Neil, put me down," Candy spit out as she pounded her fists into his back.

He smacked her butt a little harder than he meant to.

"Ouch!" She reached back and rubbed her jeans where he had hit her.

"Knock it off! I cannot believe you would get on a horse. You're pregnant with my child. You will not risk my child! Do you understand?" he said. He couldn't remember ever being so angry, but Candy had a way of pushing his buttons. At least, she used to. He had thought they were way past this.

"Neil, I've been riding since I was a kid. I wouldn't risk

the baby. I'm not stupid, and I was careful. I've never been thrown from a horse. Emily——"

He cut her off before he could finish. "Emily, I'm not your husband, I'm your brother-in-law, but maybe Brad needs to keep you a little closer to home. He certainly needs to have a talk with you about letting my wife..." He stopped. "My pregnant fiancée on a horse. She's obviously not thinking clearly, so why weren't you?"

Emily blanched as if he'd slapped her. She crossed her arms, and her blue eyes flashed with a fire he'd never seen before. "Neil, I cannot believe you would say that to me. Brad is not my keeper. He respects me. I'm his wife. Don't you ever talk to me like that again," she snapped before walking away, opening the gate and latching it behind her.

"Put me down now, Neil," Candy said, her voice shaking.

He did, and he was immediately sucker punched by the hurt and sheen of tears in her brown eyes. Her jaw quivered, and she stepped back.

"What is wrong with you, taking Emily's head off like that? She was kind enough to bring me out here, and I asked to get on the horse. She insisted on leading, as she said she didn't know my experience and I didn't know this Paint. I felt as if I was two years old, being led around on horseback when I'm probably one of the most confident riders there is. Then you come in here, dictating to me, and you hit me! How could you? I'm not your possession! You can't order me around." She started to back away, pushing back her long, dark hair, which was a tousled mess from having been tossed over his shoulder.

"Look, I'm sorry. You can't ride anymore, Candy, not when you're pregnant. That horse," Neil pointed to the Paint, who was now racing toward the herd by the feeder, "is unpredictable. You don't get on a horse unless you know something about it. I know you can ride—I've seen you. But you're not riding anymore, not while you're carrying my child!" he shouted and stepped closer to her. This time, he noticed her fisted hands, the sharp incline of her head, so he extended his hand and gave her a moment. When she turned and started toward the gate, he didn't try to touch her, because right now he was fighting the urge to shake her and toss her over his shoulder again, not letting her down until he had her back in bed. Then he'd show her who she belonged to. *Get a grip*, he told himself, taking a breath as he followed Candy back to the house. She glanced back only once, shooting him a look that said if he touched her, she'd probably deck him.

Neil wiped his jaw. When they approached the house, Brad wandered out the back door, holding the door open for Candy as she stomped inside. He shut the door and gave Neil a look, one of sympathy, but something else, too. He looked around, stepping closer to Neil and putting his hands on his hips, pushing back his tan jacket.

"You upset my wife. I got quite the earful a minute ago. You didn't really say I needed to keep Emily closer to home, did you?" He was quiet, and Neil regretted now how sharp he'd been with Emily.

"I did," he admitted. "Look, I may have overreacted a bit with your wife, but she shouldn't have let Candy get on that horse. Put yourself in my shoes. If that had been Emily, wouldn't you have reacted the same way?" he asked. The sky was gray today, and it was starting to match his mood.

"Well, it wasn't my wife on that horse. Just a word of advice, Neil—if you want Candy to be your wife, you need to dial it back a bit. Snapping like that at Emily…" Brad didn't finish. He shook his head. "Look, I understand. I probably would have reacted the same way if it had been

Emily, but you need to be more tactful." Brad reached out and gripped Neil's shoulder. "Neil, Neil, my dear brother, you've always been a voice of reason for our wives, telling me and Jed we're cavemen, running around, barking out orders, but here you are, doing the same thing. Ain't love grand?"

Neil glanced upward. Brad's words were a splash of icy water, and he didn't much care for them. He pressed his palms to the side of his head and then put them on his hips, touching his dark leather jacket. "I'll apologize to Emily," he said.

"Yeah, well, you'd best let her cool off a bit, first. Tell me, did you really toss Candy over your shoulder and spank her?" Brad had a hint of humor flashing in his eyes.

Neil didn't answer. He glanced away, and Brad laughed as he patted Neil's shoulder and started toward the barn. "Wait till I tell Jed! Oh, and be careful when you go inside. I want to have a wife I can still talk to when I come in for lunch."

Brad was still chuckling as he walked away, and as Neil opened the door, he realized he'd rather face a boardroom of sharks than the two women waiting for him on the other side.

Fifteen

"How did it go with Candy?" Emily asked, although Neil could still feel the tension between them. He'd apologized to Emily when he first walked through the back door, and she had shot him what he was pretty sure was a "Drop dead" look, though she'd been gracious enough not to make his life a living hell.

"She's not speaking to me. She locked the bedroom door and won't open it," he replied.

Emily continued to chop vegetables. He knew she was getting ready for tonight, as they were expecting his parents, as well as Jed, Diana, and their two kids. Andy and his wife, Laura, were coming as well, but only Diana and Jed were staying at the house. The rest had booked a hotel in town.

Neil pulled a knife from the block on the counter. "You got another cutting board? I'll give you a hand."

Emily pulled a second cutting board out and slid it in front of him. "Thanks. Just chop up the carrots and celery. I'll leave you the onions, too, if you'd like?" she teased.

"Yeah, sure, give me the onions. Look, I'm really sorry, Emily. I took out my frustration with Candy on you. I just reacted and didn't think. She doesn't seem to realize sometimes that her actions could get her hurt or even killed, and now that she's carrying my child, yeah, I'm worried. I always made fun of Brad and Jed, with how they acted like overly possessive men from the Dark Ages with you and Diana, but it's not so much fun when you're on the other end of it, either. I didn't really mean it, by the way, about Brad keeping you closer to home," he said as he chopped, and he didn't miss the way Emily brightened and then nudged him.

"Yes, you did mean it. It's that overprotective alpha-male thing that seems to run rampant in you Friessen men. You've just got to laugh that you're exactly like your brothers now, and you're not liking the fact that the woman you love is not toeing the line. You and your brothers would prefer if we women didn't take any chances, and if you could, each of you would keep us under your thumb. I don't think you're really sorry; I think you're sorry you weren't more diplomatic, and you're sorry for how it sounded. There's a difference," she said. She gazed up at Neil and smiled.

"So does that mean I'm still your favorite brother-in-law?" Neil asked.

She gave him an exasperated look. "Oh, Neil, you'll always have a special spot in my heart, but, now that you've shown your cards, you're just like your brothers." Emily cleared her throat and turned serious. "I've got to tell you, with Candy…" She glanced up at the ceiling. "Go easy, Neil. I can see how much you love her, but she's terrified. Being pregnant just adds to that, and the wedding… I understand what she's going through. You need to find out what she wants to do. Around the horses this morning, that was the first time I've seen her relax since she's been here. Sometimes you've got to give a little, Neil. Have you thought about all of this from Candy's viewpoint?" Emily set down her knife and stared at him, lowering her voice.

He wasn't sure if he understood what she was saying, but he also knew he'd been hurrying Candy along after years of fighting, of her hating him—or at least he thought she had. He couldn't help wanting to brand her, to say she was his, that she belonged to him. That was what marriage would mean, with his ring. His child was already growing inside her, and that took his breath away. He couldn't put those feelings into words or explain them to anyone in a way that would make sense. He met Emily's steadfast gaze. She was such a petite, soft, loving, strong woman, and she made his brother a better man, the happiest he'd ever seen him.

"Look, Candy is going to be fine," he said. If he said it, he hoped it would be enough. Even he realized she'd been jittery lately.

"Neil, I'm not so sure about that. If you keep pushing the way you are, taking over everything, telling her how to think, what to do; she's going to react like a horse would. She's going to buck or spook or something. Neil, you've taken over everything, even with this wedding."

"Emily, I've never told her how to think—"

"Yes, you have, by not asking her opinion or letting her make a decision," Emily said, interrupting him. "You even picked out her wedding dress, didn't you?"

Neil's first response was to deny everything. "Look, she didn't say what she wanted. She said it didn't matter. I just wanted to look after her, give her the best wedding."

"Neil, I'm pretty sure she's been saying loud and clear with her body language that she's freaking out. She's scared of having a child. She doesn't know us from a hill of beans. She has no family. I figured that much out, since it's only your family and friends who will be here for the wedding. She's being told where to stand, when to smile… You need to talk to her. You need to listen to her and make her tell you what she's thinking."

"How am I supposed to do that when she won't even open the door?" he said. This was an excuse, but he knew deep down that Emily was right. He'd pushed too hard.

"Oh, Neil, Neil, you surprise me; a Friessen man who doesn't know how to get a woman out of a locked bedroom!" She shook her head, and Neil realized that short of taking down the door, he was at a loss.

"Maybe I should go talk to Brad," he said.

"Or maybe you should follow me." Emily wiped her hands and set her knife in the sink, pulling open the junk drawer and rummaging around until she pulled out a Swiss Army knife.

"What are you planning on doing with that?" Neil asked as he followed her to the back stairs.

"I'm planning to open the door," she said.

Candy was curled up on the bed, staring at the door. When she first heard the footsteps on the stairs, she'd known it was Neil and had turned the lock on the doorknob, propping two pillows on the bed and watching the door. He'd first tried to turn the knob, and then he had knocked, calling out her name. Then he had pounded on the door. He hadn't given up right away, demanding that she open the door and saying she was behaving like a spoiled child. She could hear how frustrated he was with her, and he was close to yelling. He had finally given up as she clutched the pillow to her chest, waiting for him to shove the door open, but instead he had left.

This time, she heard voices, footsteps, and then something scraping the door, clicking, and the door popped open. Her mouth fell open as she spotted Emily pulling a tool from the doorknob, Neil waiting behind her.

"Thank you, Emily," he said, stepping into the bedroom.

Emily glanced at her and said, "Candy, you need to talk to him." Then she shut the door and left.

Neil crossed his arms and leaned against the door. Candy scooted up on the bed, pulling a pillow against her chest and staring back at Neil. She was not going to give in. She had a right to be angry, and she was determined to make this damn hard on him. It was unforgivable, what he had done. She was right, and he was wrong. End of story.

"Candy, I'm sorry," he said, and the way he said it started to chip away at her resolve, so she looked away and then at her hands. It was his eyes, the way he looked at her —he could make her do anything. "I know I acted… in an unforgivable way, but you scared me." He didn't move, and she could tell as he kept his arms crossed that he wouldn't stay there for long. Neil didn't wait; he made things happen, he went to people, he handled, he took charge, and that was what he'd done with her from the moment he'd rescued her when the storm hit, taking away her home and property and nearly killing her.

She flicked her gaze toward him. "How could I have scared you, Neil?"

He let out a rough laugh. "Candy, you're pregnant. You can't get on a horse when you're pregnant."

"Why?" she said. "I'm not an invalid. I'm not broken. I'm comfortable on horses. I know how to ride, and I've never in my life been thrown. I know horses. How you treated me out there wasn't okay. You humiliated me as if I was some nitwit, tossing me over your shoulder."

"I'm sorry, but I don't want you riding right now, not while you're pregnant. Can't you understand that? That horse was… unpredictable, Candy. This isn't about your ability. I know you can ride, but you didn't know anything about that horse."

She knew he was right, but she wasn't about to admit

it. The horse seemed fine, but then, she'd spent no time with it. She didn't know how it reacted to anything, and she never got on a horse unless she'd worked with it and built a connection first. She stared at her fingers again.

"Candy?" Neil prodded her gently. The floor squeaked as he walked across the room slowly and perched on the side of the bed.

"You spanked my…"

He touched her leg. "I'm sorry."

"Don't do it again."

"Okay." This time, he covered her hands with his and smoothed her fists. He moved closer so that his thigh pressed into hers. "We need to talk about the wedding," he said, somehow managing to pry her hands apart and remove the pillow she'd put between them.

"What do we need to talk about? You've already arranged everything," she said, feeling the incredible anxiety of having one more thing to buy, to be arranged, for what was supposed to have been a simple wedding.

"Well, see, that's the thing. It's been pointed out to me how I've planned this entire wedding, made all the decisions. I even picked out your dress, and not once have you said what you wanted."

This time, she really looked at Neil, and she realized she had his attention for the first time. Maybe he was finally ready to hear her. "It's a nice dress," she said.

"It's beautiful, but you could make anything lovely."

"It cost a lot of money, Neil. I didn't need anything that fancy."

"But you're worth it to me," he said.

She looked away, because he wasn't listening to her again. He didn't get what she was saying, and she didn't know how to explain it to a man who expected and wanted the best of everything.

He touched her chin and slid his fingers over her cheek. "Candy, don't do that. I want to know what you're thinking. When you turn away and say it doesn't matter, of course I'm going to decide. That's who I am. If you don't like something, you need to tell me so. You need to tell me what you want. I need to hear it."

"But I told you before, and you didn't listen to me."

"No, Candy, you never said, 'I don't like it,' or 'No, I don't want this,' or 'I want this instead,'" he said quite sharply.

Neil had a way about him of invading her space with his presence, which was so large and powerful, and letting her know he wasn't going anywhere, but he also saw things from his side only, and that was becoming clearer.

"Do you want a new dress? The wedding's tomorrow, I'll take you anywhere you want to go, and you can buy whatever you want."

"No, the dress is fine."

He let out an exasperated breath, and his jaw tightened.

"It's too late to change it anyway," she said, and he wiped his face roughly. She could tell he was struggling not to lose his temper. "I don't want an orchestra."

This time, he appeared to soften.

"Or all those fancy finger-food things and dishes from that caterer you hired. I wanted a barbecue, nothing fancy…"

Neil reached over and put his finger to her lips. "Okay, I understand. The caterer, well, it may be too late to change what we want, but if you really want the barbecue, I'll find someone to do the barbecue. The caterer will be mad; she'll have already started preparing for tomorrow."

"No, just leave the caterer. I don't want you spending any more money."

"Candy, I have the money to do this. I want you to have a wedding that you remember, that you can tell our children about. I want it to be special."

"But just having you there is all I need," she said. "I'm not comfortable with the money, Neil. I don't want everything so fancy, and no orchestra—it's too much in this small house."

"Okay, I'll cancel the orchestra, but I want music, so how about just the guitar?"

"Okay, but just one guitar. I suppose it's too late to cancel the cake and the flowers?" she asked hopefully.

He frowned as he glanced back at her. "They're bought and paid for, unless you want me to donate them to some worthy cause."

Candy groaned. "Fine, just don't buy anything else. Please."

He slid forward until they were hip to hip and leaned in, his lips so close that his warm breath heated her lips. "Nothing else; so am I forgiven?"

She slid her hand over his cheek. How could she stay mad at the first and only man to fill her dreams every night, even though he continually rode roughshod over parts of her life, making all her decisions for her when, in fact, she had a mind of her own?

"Yes…you are," she said.

He kissed her deeply until she was taking his breath as hers. She wasn't sure who moaned, but he somehow had her on her back across the bed, and he was on top of her. He pressed into her, sliding his hand over her thigh and leg, lifting it so he could slide his hand over her butt. He was so smooth and knew exactly where to touch her to ignite the burning desire she had only for him, but today he seemed hurried, or maybe it was her. In two seconds flat, he had her clothes off and tossed to the floor. Candy pulled at his shirt, and a button popped off, but she couldn't stop kissing him.

He touched every part of her, sliding his hand over her slim belly, up and over her breast, and he kissed her jaw, her neck. She wanted him so badly.

"Neil, please…" she said.

He continued down, skimming his hand over one breast while tasting the other. He was still dressed, and she yanked at the buttons on his shirt. He drew away, pulling it over his head, and she felt the chilled air over her skin. He watched her as if she were a dessert laid out just for him. Candy reached for him, and his lips met hers, and she pulled her legs up as he fit between them. She reached down to help him as he unzipped his pants and was inside her, taking both her hands, pressing them above her head, watching her as he moved so slow and deep. Then he stopped and just watched her.

"Neil, please move," she begged.

His jaw tightened as he started moving so slowly that she thought she'd go out of her mind. She tossed her head side to side until he moved faster. Candy was lost in a wave of passion that was so intense, so powerful, that she lost her reasoning. Maybe Neil knew she was going to scream or cry out, as he covered her mouth with his and moved faster. She fought to suppress her scream and moaned as he kissed her more deeply, and she felt a powerful wave of passion explode inside her, toppling her over the edge. Sex with Neil was incredible, mind blowing, and she had turned to putty in his hands.

Neil was still inside her as she lay there breathing, wrapping her arms around his back, holding him to her. She breathed in his rich male scent, which drove her to the brink of madness. She didn't know if she'd be able to catch her breath, let alone move, any time soon. All his weight was on her, pressing her into the mattress.

"Oh my God, if that's what sex is like after fighting, we should do it more often," she said.

As soon as the words left her mouth, Candy couldn't believe she'd said it, but Neil groaned, pulled out, and rolled over, taking Candy with him as he pulled the quilt over her, snuggling her against his side. She slid her leg over his still jean-clad thigh and ran her hand over the dark hair on his chest. She rested her head on his shoulder as his arm anchored her more tightly, making her feel like his possession. He was gazing up at the ceiling, not saying a word, when a honk downstairs and a commotion of voices had Candy scampering away and Neil letting her go as he slid his legs over the side of the bed, zipped up his jeans, and went to the window. He parted the curtain and looked out.

"Who's here?" she asked, covering her breasts with the edge of the quilt.

"Can't see, but I think it's Jed and Diana." Neil grabbed his shirt and started to button it before noticing the missing button. He frowned and dumped it on the chair, taking a clean red shirt from the closet and pulling it on. Candy just sat and watched, because she was absolutely terrified. Instead of seeing how freaked out she was, Neil tucked in his shirt and then leaned down and kissed her. "I'll see you downstairs," he said as he left, shutting the door behind him.

She stared at the back of the white door, her mouth open, still feeling the aftereffects of what had just transpired between them. She lay back down and pulled the covers over her head.

"So, where's the woman who managed to snag you?" Jed said as he hugged Neil and slapped his back a couple of times. Boy, did his brother look good. Neil was surprised by how much he had missed him.

"Gee whiz, couldn't you get a haircut, at least, for my wedding?" Neil teased. Jed's dark, wavy hair was long enough to cover his ears.

"Sorry, Neil. That was my fault," Diana said as she hugged Neil next. Her normally long red hair was pinned up in a haphazard bun, and she had deeper lines around her tired blue eyes. She was a new mother, her baby not even four weeks old yet, and she was still plump in the middle, looking as if she was about five months pregnant, wearing a pair of overalls over a green, long-sleeved shirt.

Just then, the baby let out a howl from the carrier Jed held. He set it on the floor and unbuckled him. "Diana, Christopher's hungry, and I can't help him."

"Oh, let me see him!" Emily said, nudging her way in and lifting the baby from the carrier. She snuggled him just as Brad came through the door with a giggling Danny tossed over his shoulder, wearing his dark blue jacket and big-boy jeans.

"Come here, you," Neil said as he reached for Danny, his two-year-old rambunctious nephew.

Danny pulled back his hood and unzipped his coat. "Uck Nee!" Danny squealed.

"That's right, that's your uncle Neil," Diana said. "Danny's been practicing most of the way here," she added as she took Christopher from Emily. Both women slipped into the living room together, and Diana lounged in one of the easy chairs. Emily handed her a pillow just as Diana unhooked a strap of her overalls and lifted her shirt to nurse the baby. Neil smiled at the sight and imagined Candy would be comfortable enough to do the same thing. He couldn't wait.

"You know what? Candy should be down in a minute. Why don't I help you bring in your luggage?" Neil said to Jed.

"Well, I was thinking about heading in to the barber for a haircut. I'll never hear the end of it when Mom gets here," Jed said, sharing a meaningful look with Diana across the room.

Brad stepped in and said something to Emily in a low voice that Neil couldn't make out. She nodded and then strode toward Jed, Brad right behind her.

"Jed, we're going to put you and Diana upstairs in the bedroom at the end of the hall," she said. "Becky's old crib is in there and ready for you."

The stairs squeaked. Neil turned and spotted Candy standing there, eyes wide, at the bottom of the stairs, as if she were hesitant to take another step. She had changed into a pair of blue jeans and a light blue shirt. She opened her mouth to say something but shut it when everyone in the room turned and stared.

* * *

CANDY WAS at a loss as she stepped off the bottom stair and stared at the three brothers, side by side. *Oh my God* was all that would come to mind. They were tall, ruggedly handsome, with square jaws, each wearing what she'd come to know as that arrogant, determined, strong Friessen expression. Maybe it was in their eyes, as the three of them, although not identical, resembled each other, and the power that exuded from them, filling the room, was enough to have Candy taking a second look. Together, they were a force that could tear a man apart—she was sure of that. What was she getting herself into?

"Oh, Candy, come and meet Diana, Jed's wife," Emily said. She thankfully must have understood Candy's plight, as she touched her arm and led her to where a redheaded woman with the brightest blue eyes was nursing a baby. The creamy white of her breast was exposed for everyone to see, and the baby was latched onto her nipple, nursing and making all kinds of squeaky noises. Candy blushed, and Diana smiled brightly.

"You must be Candy. I'd get up, but, as you can see, I've got a baby attached to my boob. I'm very happy to meet you," she said.

Candy forced herself to nod when she couldn't get her tongue to move. She couldn't help feeling as if a big old spotlight were shining down on her, and she was afraid of saying or doing something stupid. She'd have given anything to run out the back door right about then.

"You know what, Candy? That terrified look you have on

your face right now is the same one I had when I met Jed's family," Diana said. She didn't smile this time, but there was something kind and soft in her expression, something that marked her as a kindred spirit, that had Candy taking a seat on the edge of the sofa close to her, turning her back on the men.

"Jed, Brad, Neil, go and get all the luggage and take it upstairs," Emily said. "Then why don't all three of you head in to town so Jed can get his haircut? You too, Brad, and pick up the kids from school on your way home," she finished, dictating the three macho men just as little Danny raced across the floor and started bouncing in front of Candy. "And," Emily lifted the toddler and kissed his cheek, "take Danny with you, too."

Candy watched as three of the most powerful men she'd ever shared a room with fell in line and did exactly what short and petite Emily had commanded. When she inclined her head, handing Danny to Jed, the men all tromped out the door, sounding like a herd of cattle, laughing and joking. Truck doors were shut, and a vehicle started, followed by a second truck.

"How did you do that?" Candy asked as Emily and Diana shared a look.

"Oh, honey, you're marrying a Friessen man, and as strong as they are," Emily touched her head, "you need to be stronger. That's going to be our gift to you."

Emily and Diana took one look at her lost expression, and Diana said, "Candy, Neil is an amazing man; a stubborn, complex Friessen. There's nothing easy about any of them, but let me tell you, being loved by a Friessen man is worth all the difficulties and frustration they cause us. Isn't that right, Emily?" Diana inclined her head toward her sister-in-law as she moved her baby to her other breast. She must have caught some of Candy's embarrassment. Candy had never in her life sat in a room with a woman nursing a baby—and one so comfortable with exposing her breasts, at that. Candy couldn't imagine doing that and considered hiding in another room for Diana's sake.

"Candy, you know, nursing Danny, I was a wreck," Diana began. "I had to learn to get over it. He was such an exhibitionist! I tried what so many women do, draping a blanket over my shoulders so no one could see, but Danny would have none of that. He was always ripping away the blanket, pushing up my shirt, patting and playing with my breast, and Jed wasn't about to let me hide away in the bedroom. Not that we had a bunch of people coming over, but I had to get over my shyness real quick." She smiled at Candy in a way that helped her relax. "You're going to be fine, Candy." Diana pulled her shirt over her breast. "Do you mind, Emily?"

"Not at all! You give that precious boy to me," Emily said, taking the baby and holding him as he snuggled, appearing content while Diana righted her clothes and fastened her overall straps.

"Do you want me to take him back?" Diana asked.

"No, he's fine right here," Emily said as she gazed down at the baby with such longing that Candy again wondered what was wrong with her. She prayed no one offered her the baby to hold. She was terrified and not even a tiny bit intrigued.

"Candy, I'm glad the men went out and it's just us," Diana said, sharing a conspiratorial glance with Emily.

"Oh, and why is that?" Candy asked.

"So we can give you a wedding present," she answered.

Candy glanced from Emily to Diana, a bit confused and leery of receiving any more gifts. "You didn't buy me anything, did you?" she asked.

Both women laughed, but it was Diana who said, "No,

it's much better. Our wedding gift to you will be the key to handling a Friessen man."

Candy blinked before realizing these two women seemed to understand her soon-to-be husband a lot better than she did.

CHAPTER

Eighteen

T he house was alive with a commotion of voices, caterers, and vehicles. A steady buzz vibrated through the entire house, rising from downstairs.

Candy was still in bed, doing her best to sleep in. Neil had climbed out of bed, pressed a kiss to her forehead and lips, and then dressed and left, taking his tux, which had still been in the garment bag in the closet, and closing the door behind him. That had been two hours ago, and Candy was now starving but had no intention of setting one foot outside that door and facing what she was positive was a small army downstairs. Her back, however, was killing her. It was a dull throb lower down, and no matter which way she moved, she couldn't relieve the ache. She was sure it was from all the stress and anxiety of this whirlwind wedding, listening to all the information about these complex, difficult men, and being invaded last night by the entire Friessen clan, with babies and children everywhere. She'd worked herself up, and it was no wonder her back was in knots.

Their cousin, Andy, showed up at dinnertime with his

young, blonde wife, Laura, their newborn twins, and a little boy. Candy had managed to piece together that the boy wasn't Andy's but the result of a teenage pregnancy on the part of his child bride, who wasn't even of legal drinking age. On top of that, children seemed to be running everywhere, and Brad and Emily's five-bedroom, two-story home had suddenly become an overcrowded madhouse. Everyone else, including Neil's parents, who had arrived right behind Laura and Andy, seemed happy and celebratory, hugging and cooing over babies and tossing each of the rambunctious, out-of-control kids—well, in Candy's mind, anyway—around.

Candy herself had found a spot in the living room, against the wall, perched on a hard straight-back bench. Neil had joined her twice, leaving each time when one of the kids landed on him, which meant she had been left alone most of the night. Thankfully, the children seemed to have spotted her unease and steered clear.

Candy hadn't moped and pouted in the corner, though. She didn't do stuff like that. What she had done was remain polite, responding with all the right things, saying "Nice to meet you" to Laura and Andy and forcing such a phony smile on her face that everyone had to know something was wrong. Laura was quiet and seemed to be quite close with Diana and Jed. She wasn't outgoing and had been busy most of the night with nursing one baby then the other. Andy was a force of nature, darker than his cousins, with blue eyes instead of brown, but he had the same rugged, drop-dead gorgeous, magnificently sculpted body. He was the best-looking man, in a dark sort of way, that Candy had ever seen—and he terrified her.

Becky had come over once and asked if she was all right, if she needed anything. Of course, Candy had lied as if there was no tomorrow, saying she was fine. Rodney, her new father-in-law, had watched her as well from across the room.

Dinner had ended up being the barbecue Candy had wanted for the wedding, with baked beans, potatoes, salad, and what she was positive had to have been half a cow. Everyone had eaten except Candy. She had picked at her food, moving it around her plate, but the ache in her back from sitting so straight and being tense for so long was starting to bother her. To top it off, she'd had a headache that had been creeping up on her for most of the day. Neil had been happier than she'd ever seen him. Watching the brothers together with their cousin, they resembled a formidably strong pack, and any fool could see they were very much the heads of their households.

She had watched each of the women from across the room: Emily with her children, Diana with hers, and Laura always carrying around one of her babies. These women loved their families, their children, and their roles, and Candy had no doubt, by the way each of the men watched over them and their children, that the Friessens would kill anyone who tried to hurt their families. She had swallowed when the same look came into Neil's eyes from across the room. It was powerful, overwhelming, to the point that she had felt caged in. It was… freaking her out. She had swallowed, and while the children were being bathed and tucked in and everyone was distracted, Candy had slipped away to her room and shut the door. She had been lying on the bed when Neil came looking for her twenty minutes later, and this was the first time since she had found out she was pregnant that the room started spinning, and she flew off the bed, raced to the bathroom, Neil behind her, and vomited.

After that, he had tucked her in and left her to sleep, which she'd been grateful for. This morning, as she stayed in bed, her headache now gone, she dreaded getting up and facing what she imagined was the entire family, a bunch of strangers, and absolute chaos. Her stomach rumbled again, and she willed it to stop. A knock sounded at the door.

She jolted up, pulling the comforter to her chin and sitting at the edge of the bed. Neil would never knock on the door, so she fretted about who was there.

"Candy, it's Becky. Can I come in?"

"Um, I'm not really decent," she called out.

Becky didn't listen but opened the door, and Candy scooted up further on the bed. Emily and Diana followed Becky in, one carrying a breakfast tray and the other coffee. Candy swept back her tangled hair. She had to look pretty bad, but at least she wasn't naked, as she'd slept in one of Neil's t-shirts.

"This is your wedding day," Emily said. "I know you weren't feeling well last night, but I thought with all the commotion downstairs, you might like breakfast in your room." She set the tray on Candy's lap. There was a plate of scrambled eggs, sausage, and toast, with a small fruit salad.

"Thank you," Candy said, but she couldn't look at them. Even this morning, she was uncomfortable around these people. They were so close. They were a family, and she didn't understand how she could ever fit in. Her stomach was still bothering her, cramping off and on, but it was more of a discomfort, probably because she was so hungry and Neil hadn't let her do much of anything all week. She was usually active, and she never sat around doing nothing, ever. She loved hard labor, lifting and carrying things, shoveling dirt and manure, lifting hay bales and buckets, fixing anything, and especially riding her horse. Maybe that was why her muscles were going soft from weeks of doing very little, lifting nothing, and spending most of her time with Neil in bed.

"Are you feeling okay this morning? Neil said you were sick last night and had a headache, too," Emily said. Diana hovered behind her in a pair of black sweats and a blue sweatshirt.

"Yeah, I just… sorry about last night. I didn't feel well, but I'm okay now," Candy said. She wondered for a second whether her nose was growing from the bold-faced lie.

"You poor baby, getting pounced on by Neil's family, all the kids running around last night. Why don't you just take it easy, have some breakfast? Everything is being taken care of. You don't have to do anything. What time is the hairdresser coming, Emily?" Diana asked.

Emily glanced at her watch and missed the alarm that had to be showing on Candy's face. One thing Candy knew was that she had the worst poker face ever.

"You didn't know a hairdresser was coming, did you?" Becky asked, and her mouth widened as she groaned and shook her head. "That son of mine."

"I can do my own hair. Or is Neil worried I'm not going to look good enough?" Candy snapped. The instant the words were out of her mouth, she regretted having said them out loud.

"Of course you can." Emily glanced up at Diana, who sucked in her bottom lip, sharing a sympathetic look with Candy.

"You know what, Candy? This is your wedding day. You tell us what you want, and we'll make it happen for you. If you don't want a hairdresser, we'll send her away. We'll bar your door and make sure no one gets in. You want us to get rid of anyone, tell us right now. Consider us your personal slaves for the day. Anything you want, you shall have," Diana said, leaning over to pat Candy's leg under the blanket.

"So when the hairdresser shows, you'll tell her to go away?"

"Yes," all three women said in unison, their faces showing their solidarity. "And the makeup artist, too," Emily added.

"He hired a makeup artist, are you serious?" Candy blurted out, staring with disbelief at all three women.

"She's downstairs now," Diana said before clearing her throat.

The warm eggs and sausage had started to give off an odor that was turning Candy's stomach. It ached and cramped.

"Here, let me move that," Emily said, lifting the tray from her lap and setting it on the dresser. "Why don't you try some toast to settle your stomach?" She set the small plate on her lap, and Candy took a bite.

"What else has Neil arranged to surprise me today?" Candy asked, and the women shared a look that had Candy saying, "What else could there be?"

"He hired the lady from the bridal shop to help you get dressed," Diana said.

Candy knew her jaw was hanging open, as she could feel the muscle stretch, and she shut it as she looked away. She started to say something but, for the life of her, wasn't sure what to say.

"And an aesthetician to give you a manicure and pedicure," Emily added.

"I'll get rid of them," Diana said, turning to the door.

"They're here now?" Candy asked.

"Having coffee with Neil," Emily said. She glanced up at Becky and winced.

"So is this what you meant about me standing my

ground with Neil, not letting him push me around or arrange me, to stand up to him until he tells me all that he's hiding? I've got to tell you, I don't know how you do it. Watching you all last night, it looked more like the men have you where they want you," Candy said. She wasn't being very diplomatic, but the art of handling a difficult man who could bark orders and kill a man for looking at her the wrong way wasn't coming easily for her.

"Well, that's where you're wrong, Candy. I love my children. That's where I want to be, and my husband has my back, always, so I don't ever have to worry about someone coming up and shoving a knife in it again," Diana said a little sharply. She flushed. "Sorry, but each of us is happy. We told you that you can't hold back with Neil. If we did that with our husbands, they'd steamroll right over us. You're being diplomatic, loving, and pleasantly persistent, but at times you need to fight back," Diana said, quite clearly making her point.

"So what am I doing wrong?" Candy asked, feeling like a failure.

All three women shared another meaningful look. "You can't let Neil take over. You need to step in and handle details. If you want a barbecue and not a caterer, you need to arrange it. You need to tell him, no, you'll pick out your own dress, and then pick up the phone yourself and handle it," Becky said.

"When you hesitate or you're not sure, they sense weakness, and they'll swoop in and take over," Emily added.

"Okay, enough," Becky said. "Candy, you need to eat something. Diana won't let anyone else upstairs unless you give the go-ahead. You're getting married today, and after that you'll learn how to handle your husband."

Emily picked up the tray and set it on Candy's lap. "Eat what you can."

"Okay, so tell us what you want us to do," Diana said, sounding like an excited little kid.

Candy scooped up a forkful of eggs and chewed. For the first time, she felt that someone other than Neil truly had her back. She had a lot to learn and a lifetime to learn it.

"Tell Neil I said to send everyone away except the hairdresser," Candy said.

Diana winked at her and said, "That's my girl."

Nineteen

"You look beautiful," Diana said as she put both of her hands on Candy's bare shoulders. Candy was resting on a chair in Emily's large master bedroom, where the women had ushered her after she finished eating. Apparently, Neil hadn't argued when Diana relayed Candy's demand for a hairdresser only.

Candy had enjoyed a nice, leisurely bath in Emily's en suite bathroom. The women had been true to their word and kept everyone away, and for the first time since being here, Candy breathed a sigh of relief. Now, dressed in the beautiful white gown Neil had picked out, with a clasp around her neck and a deep V that accentuated a generous amount of cleavage, she felt sexy, desired, and beautiful. Maybe Neil had been right about the dress.

The hairdresser had pinned the lace veil to her dark curls along with six white roses, and Candy had to admit she looked stunning. She did, in fact, feel like a princess. Emily wore a long burgundy dress with a lace bodice and straight skirt, while Diana wore a short, green, sleeveless dress, tight around her stomach and her breasts. The color really brought out her eyes. Becky stood behind her, wearing a light blue beaded silk top with a matching skirt. There was a knock on the door, and Emily firmed her lips, opening it a crack to see who it was. Candy couldn't see, but she heard a man's voice. *Brad,* she thought, and then Emily shut the door, holding a lovely bouquet of pink roses and white lilies.

"Everyone is downstairs whenever you're ready, Candy," Emily said. She gestured to Diana and Becky, and they started toward the door.

"Wait," Candy said. "I don't have anyone to stand up for me. Emily, Diana, I know Neil suggested both of you, and he probably even asked you already for me, but would you do it? I know I didn't plan this very well."

"Now, stop right there. You were overwhelmed," Diana said.

"And you had your hands full, trying to keep your wits about you with a Friessen man," Emily said.

"Don't forget that you were trying to keep your sense of self," Becky added. "My sons are honorable, strong, solid men, but you need to keep your head together and learn to stand your ground."

"And... Neil already asked us," Emily and Diana muttered.

"I guess I haven't done too good a job of standing up to Neil," Candy said.

"Oh, honey, you've got that man twisted up in knots right now," Becky said. "He loves you, but you make sure he understands he can't decide for you, that you have a mind of your own, because if you don't speak up, he won't wait. He'll take the reins, and one day you're going to wake up and realize that your man is running your life, and you'll no longer be you."

Candy watched Becky and wondered for a minute, by the way she had said it, if she spoke from experience.

"Well, I would love to stand up for you," Diana said.

"So would I," Emily added.

Candy stood up and winced from the ache in her shoulder. She rolled it a bit and saw the concern on Emily's face.

"You okay?" she asked.

"Yeah, fine. Just stiff, is all, from not doing anything, and, I guess, the joys of being pregnant." That was what she told them, but she wondered whether she would feel unwell and achy throughout this entire pregnancy. When she got out of the bath, she had noticed she was spotting, but instead of worrying, she'd dismissed it. She didn't want to inconvenience anyone. That was what she had told herself as she put it from her mind.

"I'm ready," Candy said.

"Well, let's go then." Becky opened the door and signaled to someone just as what sounded like a dozen guitars started strumming the wedding march.

"Neil!" they all muttered as they burst out laughing.

Twenty

The entire house had been transformed into what could have been a page from a bridal magazine. The living room furniture had been arranged tastefully to the side so that an archway of flowers, where Candy and Neil were to stand, could be the centerpiece of the room. The dining room, which was just off the living room through a set of double glass doors, held a champagne fountain and warming trays filled with enough hors d'oeuvres and platters of food to feed a small army. The aroma was mouthwatering, and with all the mountains of flowers, the house had never smelled better. There were bows and decorations, and Brad and Jed stood beside Neil in their dark suits. Andy stood with Laura, holding one of their babies in the crook of his arm, and Laura held the other sleeping baby. Gabriel, her son, was pasted to Andy's leg, wearing a white shirt, dress pants, and a tie. He beamed up at Andy, and Neil was taken aback and almost brought to tears by the change in his cousin since he'd last seen him, after Jed's surgery.

Neil watched as his bride came down the stairs first,

followed by Diana and Emily, who held up the train and helped Candy down. Neil had to suck in his breath, as he was bowled over by how stunning Candy was. She accepted the bouquet from Emily, looked up, and met Neil's gaze as he watched her, willing her toward him. She lifted her skirt, and Emily and Diana straightened the train that flowed behind the stunning gown before taking their spots up front. The guitarists continued to play in the background as Candy started toward Neil. When she reached his side, she handed Emily her bouquet, and Neil took her hands. He noticed there were a few beads of sweat above her brow. It wasn't that hot in the room—cozy and warm, maybe, but not hot enough for him to sweat—so he wondered if it was just her nerves.

"You okay?" he whispered.

She offered him a quick smile and nodded rather sharply. "Yeah."

Neil turned to the minister, a tall, thin, dark-haired man with a collar, and said, "Let's begin."

Then Candy stumbled, her face went pale, and she cried out, clutching his hand as she keeled over.

Ignoring the commotion from everyone else, Neil was on his knees. "Candy, talk to me, honey!"

She tossed her head slowly from side to side. Her eyes were glazed and open but didn't appear to be registering anything. Her breathing was shallow, with beads of sweat on her forehead and upper lip, and the color in her face paled.

"She's bleeding," Emily said with a gasp as she lifted Candy's skirt. Neil glanced at her skirt and the floor, which was stained with blood. Everyone was talking, hurrying, and someone was beside him. It was Diana, and she set towels under Candy.

"There's a lot of blood here," Diana said. "She must be miscarrying."

"I'm calling an ambulance," Brad said sharply.

Jed touched Neil's shoulder just as Danny started crying, and another child fussed. They were scared, and someone started organizing and ushering the kids out.

Brad hurried back, the phone to his ear. "Ambulance is ten minutes out. They said to raise her legs, get them elevated."

"Neil, you can't wait. She's bleeding too much," Becky said.

Jed grabbed his keys, and Emily kneeled down with a blanket. Neil was holding Candy's trembling hand, her teeth chattering.

"She's going into shock, Neil!"

He didn't know who had said it, but he lifted her with the blanket. Emily helped by holding the dress as he hurried to the door. Jed was running to his truck and had it backed up to the door, while Rodney held the door open. It seemed everyone was helping. Neil climbed into the truck, and Candy was lifted on his lap, a blanket on top of her. Everyone was talking at once, and all he could see was Candy's pale face, her eyes distant right before they fluttered closed.

CHAPTER
Twenty~One

Neil couldn't remember ever having felt so helpless. Even through the storm with Candy, keeping her safe over and over, nothing compared to holding her on his lap as she hemorrhaged and went limp in his arms. Even when she had fallen into that hole after the storm, when she was running from him, the icy terror he had felt then had nothing on this.

Jed had driven fast and furious, blasting his horn as he swerved around slow drivers, crossing the center line over and over as he pulled up to the emergency doors of Well Grey Hospital. Those had been the longest ten minutes of Neil's life.

The emergency personnel raced out with a gurney, pulling Neil's door open before Jed could stop.

"What happened?" a doctor asked as Neil set Candy on the gurney.

"She just collapsed. She's pregnant. Is she losing the baby?" he shouted as he ran beside the gurney. Candy was wheeled into a room, and a monitor appeared. Her gown was cut off, and there was so much blood. That gorgeous dress was ruined. There was yelling and orders, and then a nurse touched Neil's arm and said, "You have to leave."

He started to say no, but the doctor barked, "Get him out of here!"

"Type match her blood," he heard someone saying. Then the door was shut, and he just watched through the glass, staring at all the blood and at how still Candy was.

"Neil, sit down. They'll come out and tell us what's going on as soon as they know something," Jed said, sliding his arm around Neil's shoulder as he squeezed and then hugged him.

Neil allowed himself a moment to lean on Jed as he fought the sting of tears burning the back of his eyes. He felt completely hollowed out inside, and somehow Jed directed him to sit in one of the vinyl padded seats in the waiting area. It was then that he looked down at his bare hands, stained with blood, Candy's blood. His white shirt and tux jacket were stained, as well, ruined. He pulled on the bow tie and undid his top button so he could breathe, and he noticed Jed had already tossed his coat aside and rolled up the sleeves of his white shirt, loosened his tie.

"So what do you think happened?" Jed asked, standing in front of him.

The waiting room was filled with people, young and old. He couldn't sit here and wait, so he got up and started pacing, running his hands through his hair and picking up the metallic scent of blood.

"I don't know. I know she wasn't feeling well last night. She had a headache, threw up. I thought it was just nerves. She was overwhelmed by the family." He paused. "Oh my God. I just realized—maybe I hurt her. I tossed her over my shoulder yesterday after I found her on a horse. I hauled her off and spanked her. I was so mad. What if I did this?" Neil was rambling, and a few people in tube waiting room gave him a look. They had obviously heard.

Jed didn't smile, but there was something in his eyes when he glanced away and then back again. "Doubt that, Neil. What is it with our women? Don't know how many times Diana did the same thing. Horses and pregnant women don't mix. Did you really spank her?"

"Well, I smacked her bottom while she was over my shoulder. It wasn't a spanking, geez. Don't turn me into one of those guys. I just lost it," he said.

"Well, I gotta tell you that what you did, I've thought of doing more times than I'll ever admit. Don't tell Diana. I've had to walk away, but Diana… she pushes it a lot. She's a stubborn woman. I worry about her sometimes." Jed tapped Neil's shoulder. "Doctor's coming."

Neil stood up, fully alert, as the doctor approached. He was older, a little round in the middle, gowned up, with blood spattered on his shirt.

"You're the young woman's husband?" he asked, moving Neil into the hallway away from the others. Jed stood beside him.

"Yes," he said, very aware they weren't technically married.

"Your young wife had an ectopic pregnancy. The tube ruptured, and she's on her way to emergency surgery. She lost a lot of blood. We had to give her two units already."

"I don't understand. What does 'ectopic' mean? Is the baby okay? Did she lose it?" Neil was frantic.

"It's one of those things that just happen. It was never a viable pregnancy. The egg sometimes implants in the ovarian tube instead of the womb. Her ovarian tube ruptured, and I'm afraid there was no way to save the baby.

There are other complications, as well." He touched Neil's shoulder and guided him around the corner so no one could hear.

Neil felt a sharp ache inside his chest at the mention that his child was gone. He'd gotten used to the idea of being a father. He wanted children so badly. This was a blow he hadn't expected. He had everything to provide for his children: money, status, love. He had so much love to give his child. Candy was going to be devastated. He had to clear his throat to be able to speak. It helped to have Jed there.

Jed must have known, because he put his hand on Neil's shoulder and asked, "What complications? Is Candy all right?" He squeezed Neil's shoulder, and it was the anchor and support Neil needed as he crossed his arms over his chest.

"Can I see her?" he asked.

"I'm sorry. She's being prepped for emergency surgery. I'll have someone update you. Just be prepared for the possibility that we may not be able to save the fallopian tube, not with this amount of bleeding."

The doctor walked away to the elevator just as the doors opened and Neil's family stepped out. Everyone was still in their good clothes except for Diana and Emily, who both wore jeans. All of them had such worried expressions.

His mother was the first to reach him, and she hugged him as if he were still her little boy. He held her tight as his emotions got the better of him, and for the first time since he was a kid, he wept.

CHAPTER
Twenty~Two

After three hours of sitting in the surgical waiting room, Diana was the first to leave, going home to nurse Christopher and help out Laura, who, along with their neighbor, June, had stayed with the kids. Andy and Jed sat across from Neil, chatting and taking turns pacing with him. Brad and Rodney sat on either side of Neil, and he could feel their support. Brad had long since ripped off his tie, shed his suit jacket, and rolled up his sleeves. He was so much like Jed. The two of them lived in their scruffy jeans and hated wearing anything formal. Neil could go either way, and he enjoyed days and nights of dressing up in his finest. It was who he was, and for so long he'd pictured Candy beside him. His dream had evolved over the weeks they'd been together, and he pictured her on his arm, drama free, so down to earth and real. He finally had her, and it was tearing him up inside to think he could lose her before they'd even started their lives together.

"Neil," Andy said, gesturing to a man in scrubs fast approaching. Everyone stood up and surrounded him.

"She's stable" was the first thing the doctor said as he looked up at the men surrounding him.

Neil felt like weeping, and he heard everyone murmur sighs of relief. Someone patted his back, and Brad said, "Good news, Neil."

"We've removed her ruptured fallopian tube. There was no saving it, and we had to control the bleeding, but we ran into a problem. Even after we took it out, we couldn't stop the hemorrhage. We had no choice but to do a hysterectomy."

Neil wasn't sure he'd heard the doctor right, but he heard a gasp behind him that barely registered. Then someone said, "When can he see Candy?"

His head was spinning as he tried to understand what the doctor had just said. "You did a hysterectomy?" he said, voice gruff.

"I'm sorry. We didn't have a choice," the doctor said. "If we'd seen her sooner, we could have taken other steps. We don't know how long it's been since it ruptured. She was already bleeding internally. Generally, there are signs beforehand, symptoms: cramping, discomfort, shoulder pain. If we'd seen her earlier, an ultrasound would have picked it up. I'm sorry."

"She's alive, Neil. That's all that matters," Brad said.

Neil shrugged off his hand and stepped away, wiping his mouth between his thumb and forefinger. "So we can't have kids, but she was pregnant. We wanted children. If you'd seen her sooner, she'd still have her uterus, and then she could still get pregnant." Neil knew he wasn't making any sense.

"Son, you need to take some time. Take a minute," Rodney said, resting his large, wrinkled hand on Neil's shoulder.

"I need some air," Neil said as he walked away.

IT HAD STARTED TO RAIN, and not one of those light rains. It poured, and Neil stood outside the hospital, soaked, as the rain poured on him. His tux, his shirt, everything was pasted to his skin as the water poured around him. He blinked and watched the rain pound the concrete. Puddles were forming, and the water was running in streams into the gutter. He could smell the underlying scent of rotting leaves, dirt, and vegetation that only a hard rain could stir up, but eventually the earth would be clean and fresh for a new beginning.

There was a chill in the air, and he was cold. He hissed steam as he struggled to breath. He couldn't think. His mind was racing, so he just watched people running to their cars, newspapers over their heads, hoods up, some with umbrellas. A few glanced his way, and then an umbrella appeared over his head. He glanced behind him and was surprised that Andy was there, holding it.

"I need a minute" was all Neil could say. He wasn't interested in playing nice, especially with Andy.

"Take all the time you need," Andy said.

Neil glanced back at Andy with the shrewdness that often appeared in his expression. "Did you hear what the doctor said?" he asked. His throat was thick and scratchy. Neil wasn't an emotional man. He was passionate, he was strong, he was a Friessen. But this was not in his plan, and Neil was a planner. He was an organizer. He made things happen. He didn't know how to adjust his perfectly outlined marriage-and-baby plan and mold it into something different with this curveball he'd just been thrown.

"I heard."

"So what am I supposed to do with this? Come on, Andy, what would you do?" Neil crossed his arms and continued to watch the water pound the pavement. He glanced over at the sympathy in Andy's light blue eyes.

"I can't tell you what to do, Neil. This is your life. I honestly don't know what I'd do, and my situation is entirely different," Andy said.

Neil watched his cousin, a man who had surprised the hell out of him, marrying Laura the way he had. Neil knew that in the beginning, Andy had done so out of obligation over her circumstances, but even now, after they had reconciled and Andy had stepped away from his family on his own, Neil could see he loved her. He was carving out his own way for the first time in his life, with newborn twins that Neil would have given his right arm to have. "How are things going with you and Laura?" he asked.

Andy let out a soft chuckle and flashed a grin that Neil hadn't seen before. "Pretty good, actually, considering…" He let his words trail off and then shook his head, which was so like him. He held on to everything, good or bad, and sometimes Neil wondered where he was or what he was up to.

"Considering what?" Neil asked.

"She's young. She's been through a lot. She wants to go back to school. She never finished high school, getting pregnant with Gabriel. I mean, she dropped out, got a job to support him," Andy said.

"Well, good for her," Neil said, wishing it was more of a distraction for him, but then he noticed the way Andy didn't seem enthusiastic. "Are you kidding me, Andy? She wants to go back to school and you don't want her to? Let me guess. You want her in your bed, raising your children at home. You want to tell her what to do, how to think?" Neil snapped. He was angry at the crap life had just dealt him, and he was taking it out on Andy.

"Exactly what you're doing here, cos. Don't think I

didn't notice. I listen. A lot has happened to you over the past week, and the family hasn't missed how you're exactly like Brad, Jed, and myself. We just don't make excuses. You arranged everything for your lady, even bought her dress, bossing her around, tossing her over your shoulder. I heard it, so don't go throwing back at me what a selfish bastard you think I am. I am selfish, because I do want my wife at home with my children. I want to take care of her, handle things for her, and you were doing exactly the same thing." Andy said it so matter-of-factly that Neil actually bared his teeth.

"You bastard," he barked out, but he was really saying it about himself, because Andy was right. He was just like his cousin.

"I never said I wasn't," Andy replied. "I've never tried to be anything different. Laura knows I'm not going to change, and there are things she doesn't need to know. She needs protecting, and I intend to do just that for her. Can you not say the same thing?" he asked.

Neil watched Andy and wondered if his cousin knew everything he'd done. Could he read his mind and know the secrets he'd kept from Candy? Her property wasn't gone—he had bought it. She just didn't know it yet. He planned to tell her eventually. He was just waiting for the right time. He'd kept her out of the loop and away from anyone who could have hinted that some local had bought her property, because then she would have asked questions, and that he couldn't have; not with the resort he wanted to build still on the backburner in his mind. Neil was aware she wouldn't forgive him if he went ahead and started building.

"I had plans, you know," Neil said. "I've wanted her for so long, but I thought she hated me. My God, she's the only woman who ever had me at hello, stumbling around like a fumbling first-timer. I know how to woo women, could have had any woman I wanted, but I wanted her. She didn't give a crap about flash and glitter and money or how big the rock was that glittered from her finger. She was uncomfortable with my money, with my power. She was barely scraping by. I watched. I knew, but I couldn't help her. She wouldn't take anything from me. She hated me, or so I thought, until that storm hit and I found her pinned down and hurt. She would have died there for her animals, the horses, that floppy-eared pain-in-the-ass donkey," he snapped. Neil didn't miss the look of amusement in Andy's gaze. "Don't ask."

Andy still appeared amused as he nodded.

"She didn't have anything," Neil continued. "She was so far in the hole that the bank owned her property, and they had foreclosed. I bought it only because I found out some rich developer had put in an offer and was planning on building condos up and down the beach. It would have killed her."

"I can see how you wouldn't like that too much if you wanted the property."

"Yeah, well, that's true. I wasn't interested in having all that construction and all those people right beside our property. I wouldn't have any control, and some prick would be flaunting his success right up my nose. This seemed like the easiest solution, although Candy wouldn't have seen it that way at the time. I do plan on telling her. I just didn't know how to do it without her thinking I planned it. I had every intention of just letting the bank keep it. That land was the one thing that came between us over and over, and I thought if it was gone, she'd know I only wanted her. The problem is that she believes it's really gone," Neil said with a sigh.

"Oh, I see." Andy still held the umbrella over both

their heads. "I understand where you're coming from, if it's any consolation, and I may not be the right person to be asking. I have my own secrets that I've been holding on to and haven't told Laura. They affect her, and they'd hurt her. I don't want her to know."

He was so matter of fact, but Neil studied the troubled expression on his cousin's face, as if Andy were trying to convince himself his decision was sound. Andy had always been in Neil, Brad, and Jed's shadow. He resembled them, and even his dark hair had the same natural waves as Jed's, though he had kept it clipped short, neat, and rich-looking until lately. There had always been something colder about him that didn't fit into the close, warm relationship that Neil had with Jed and Brad. But then, Andy had grown up alone, and with parents like Caroline and Todd, it was a wonder he hadn't turned out to be cold and calculating like them.

No, Andy had a conscience, and that was why he was here and probably why Neil was listening to him. Neil himself had a shrewd, ruthless side that he tapped into for his own business dealings, although he'd never admit it to anyone.

"What now, Andy?" he asked.

"Only you can decide that, Neil. You got dealt a shitty hand."

"I want kids. Lots of them," he said.

"I know."

"I want my own. My God, I had already planned it, how many, and I could imagine her belly swollen with my child. We'd have lots, and they'd have her dark hair. You know what? I imagined her nursing my child from her breast. She would have been a wonderful mother. She just didn't know it, but if you'd seen her with her animals, the caring, the love… She'd give her life for them, and she'd have done the same for our children."

"You need to ask yourself if she can be enough," Andy said. "Do you love her enough? You know, I know better than anyone that sometimes when you make a plan, life changes everything and you have to go to plan B, and sometimes you end up having to throw that plan right out the window, too, and then scramble for plan C, which really isn't any type of plan at all. It sometimes comes down to doing what you can with what you've got," he finished, speaking from the heart.

As Neil watched his cousin, it was the first time he noticed his expression, one of old wisdom only possessed by people who had clawed their way out of the slums, getting kicked in the head over and over until they became smarter, self-made men with skeletons stuffed in their closets. "Sounds like you're speaking from experience there, cos."

"Maybe, but this is about you and your girl, who's lying up there in a hospital bed." He nodded toward the hospital and noticed Brad making a beeline straight for them. He wore his suit jacket, his tie undone, his hair soaked and plastered to his head.

"She's awake," Brad said, wearing an expression of concern for Neil. "Emily's in with her, but she's been asking for you. What do you want me to tell her?"

"Nothing," Neil said.

Both men glanced at him. For the first time since he could remember, Brad looked as if he wanted to knock him around. Andy wore an unreadable expression as he glanced at Brad. "It's his choice, Brad. Only he can make it," he said.

"Yeah, well, there's a young lady up there who's just had her world ripped apart. She's scared out of her mind, and she's not as tough as you think she is, Neil," Brad barked.

"What the hell kind of asshole do you think I am?" Neil spat out. "I'm going up." He stopped and then stepped back to his cousin, reaching out to shake his hand. "Thank you, Andy."

"For what?" Andy said, gripping Neil's hand.

"For what you said. For listening. For being an asshole, too. I guess we're alike in more ways than I'd hoped."

Andy didn't say anything else, and Brad watched them with a bit of amusement and curiosity. Neil didn't wait around to explain but strode through the puddles, aware that his eight-hundred-dollar shoes were now ruined.

Neil waved his mother away when he stepped out of the elevator.

Her eyes widened, and she firmed her lips and said, "Well, the least you could do is get a towel from the nurse and dry off a bit before you go in. You're dripping everywhere."

Jed strode past his mother to the nurses' station, said something and gestured to Neil, and then walked back over. "Here's a towel. Did you clear your head?"

"In a way. Candy's awake, I heard. How's she doing?" Neil didn't miss the strange expression shared between Jed and his mother right before Rodney strode down the hall and jabbed his finger at Neil.

"You need to go take care of your bride," his father said as he stepped closer. "Emily's with her now."

"Well, how is she?" Neil asked his father, knowing darn well he was stalling.

"How would you feel if you woke up surrounded by a bunch of people who are still strangers to you, expecting to see your husband there but seeing he's the only one who's not?"

"We're not married, Dad. Remember, this happened before she said 'I do,'" Neil said, receiving surprised looks from Jed, his mom, and his dad, except no one was more surprised by what he'd just said than he was.

"I hope you're a little more polished than that before you head in," his father said in a strong voice that Neil hadn't heard since he was a teenager, after his dad had caught him fooling around with a high school cheerleader, her top off, with plans to go a little further than just touching and petting.

The elevator dinged behind him, and a sopping wet Brad and Andy stepped out.

"Excuse me," Neil said as he stepped around his father. Rodney wore a sudden expression of disapproval, and Neil didn't like it at all.

Neil had forgotten to ask what room Candy was in, and he was thankful when he spotted Emily coming out halfway down the hall.

She looked up and waved to him. "Neil, glad you're here. She's waiting for you," she said.

"Yeah, well… how is she?" It was all he could think of asking, and he'd asked everyone except Candy. Maybe Emily sensed his apprehension, his nervousness, his anger, and his concern. He was still struggling to hold it together.

She touched his hand. "Just go be with her. Just tell her you love her. She's scared and devastated, and she feels so alone. Oh, we were all there, but it was you she wanted, even though she wouldn't say it. I've seen that broken look before. I had it once myself. Before you go in there, Neil, you should know she blames herself."

"For what?" Neil said, his throat thick and scratchy.

"For losing the baby, for not being able to give you children now, for everything. She's not making a lot of sense. You need to go talk to her and tell her it doesn't matter."

Neil had an unreadable poker face, and he prided himself on it. This was a good thing, because to him, it did matter.

Apparently his poker face wasn't as good as he thought, though, as Emily raised her eyebrows and said, "Oh, I see. Well, don't hurt her," before she walked away.

Neil pushed the door open, taking in the sterile white walls, the single hospital bed, and a cheap small television that was so bulky it had to be twenty years old, if not more. He looked everywhere except at the women lying quiet and still in the hospital bed. He could smell the antiseptic cleaner the hospital used, but he could also smell Candy's vanilla-scented shampoo. It was faint, but it was what drew his gaze to her.

She was watching him, though her beautiful dark eyes, which always seemed to be tinged with a ring of fire, were now filled with such sadness. There was something broken in the way she watched him and lay there with not an ounce of fight in her.

"Hey, how are you feeling?" he asked, very aware of the distance between them.

"Okay," she muttered, her voice gruff and sounding very tired. She didn't reach for him. In fact, she kept her hand fisted beside her pillow, her long dark hair draped in a tangled mess. The roses and veil had been plucked out, and the pins, too, but her hair was still a mass of curls. Her face was pale, and she had not a stitch of makeup on.

Neil could feel the awkwardness, and he noticed the way she rested her hand over her stomach as he took another step closer.

"I'm sorry, Neil."

"For what? Why are you sorry?" he said. He touched

the steel bed rail, noticing the IV tube running into her arm and a spot of blood over the clear tape where it went into the back of her hand.

A tear slid down her cheek. She swiped it away. "For ruining your day." She wouldn't look at him when she said it.

"You didn't ruin my day. My God, woman, you damn near died! You scared the hell out of me again. Why didn't you tell me there was something wrong? Last night I found you, and then you were sick. I should have brought you to the hospital last night," he said, looking down on her as she flicked her gaze to him, but he still hadn't touched her.

"If you mean not feeling well because I was pregnant, how was I supposed to know? I've never been pregnant before. How do I know what's normal, what's not? Besides, it's a moot point now," she said, still not looking at him.

"Candy, the doctor mentioned cramping, shoulder pain."

She worried her lower lip between her teeth, and he could tell she was hiding something.

"Seriously, Candy…" He let out a sigh when she scrunched her face. "Why wouldn't you tell me? My God, I would have brought you right in and gotten you help. They wouldn't have had to do a hysterectomy," he snapped. He hadn't meant it to come out so sharply, and he realized, as she softly wept, what a bastard he was being. "Candy, I'm sorry. I didn't mean to say that."

She sniffed loudly, her face wet. "Yes, you did, because you blame me. I knew you did when I woke up and you weren't there. It was your dad and mom, Emily, Brad, Jed, they were all here. Emily had to tell me…" Her voice choked on a sob. "She had to tell me that I lost the baby, that they had to do a hysterectomy to save me." She was having trouble catching her breath, and she put her hand over her abdomen and winced as she tried to inhale.

"Are you hurting? Did they give you anything for the pain?"

She shook her head, and as he went to touch her hand, she pulled away and seemed to withdraw into herself. "I was spotting before the wedding, but I didn't know what was wrong…" she sobbed.

Neil shut his eyes and had to count so he didn't yell at her. Spotting, seriously? How could she not have said anything? He jabbed his hand in his hair as she sobbed and sniffed. "Look, let me call the nurse. I'll have her get you something for the pain."

"No, I've had enough. I'm tired. I'd like to go to sleep," she said.

"Fine," he said, watching how stiff she became. "Do you want me to stay?" It was so awkward between them that he didn't know what to say. What he really wanted to do was shake her.

"No, you should go. You probably have a lot to do at Brad's, with the caterers, the guests. You should go and look after that."

Neil studied her, and maybe he felt some relief or something, as he found himself bending over. Instead of kissing her lips, he pressed a kiss to her forehead, and he felt her wince. Maybe she really didn't want him here, or maybe she knew how furious he was.

"I'll see you later, then. Get some rest," he said. As he touched the door and pulled it open, he glanced back only once, and he left.

CHAPTER

Twenty~Four

Candy lay in that narrow hospital bed, watching Neil walk out the door without looking back, and for the first time in her life, she felt her heart break in two. She'd never been so emotionally connected to a man, but Neil had walked into her life, scooped her off the ground, protected her, and kept her safe in a way she'd never expected. She'd thought he only wanted her land, but when he had come for her during that storm, when she was at the lowest point in her life, her heart had cracked open, and she'd let him in.

Now she saw his hesitation. When she had opened her eyes, groggy and confused, she had expected Neil to be there holding her hand. But he wasn't. It was Emily. The rest of the family hovered, and she saw their concern when she asked for Neil and where he was, the expression on Jed's face and then on Brad's.

She was tired and would have loved nothing more than to curl up and sleep, never to wake up again, all because the emptiness burning a hole in her heart was stronger than the drugs they'd given her.

The door was pushed open, and Candy's heart leapt with joy, as Neil must have had a change of heart. Except it was only Emily. Her hair was still styled, and she looked so pretty with the makeup on her fresh complexion. She didn't hesitate one second as she stepped toward the bed, and Candy couldn't stop her lips from trembling. The sob broke free and choked her.

Emily petted her hair, rubbed her arm, and just said, "It's okay. Everything's going to be okay."

"I thought you were Neil, coming back," Candy cried.

"He said you were tired, wanted to sleep. I was just coming in to check on you."

"I just told him that because he didn't want to be here. He blames me, Emily."

"No, he doesn't blame you. Why would you think that? He's scared, is all." Emily rubbed her arm and then grabbed a handful of Kleenex on the nightstand to wipe Candy's face. The tears, still streaming, were making her skin extremely sensitive. Her nose was running, and she took the Kleenex and blew loudly. She was lying on her side, a pillow supporting her back, another at her belly.

"I missed all the signs," she said. "I tried to tell him I didn't know what to expect, what was normal and what wasn't. He asked about cramping, shoulder pain. I had that. I started spotting before I got dressed, but I put it out of my mind. I didn't want to disappoint Neil." Her voice caught, and Emily stood close with such empathy in her expression, just listening to her. She had no judgment at all, and Candy felt safe talking with her.

"I haven't been feeling well all week. I thought it was nerves. I mean, I'd just found out I was pregnant. I hadn't even seen a doctor. I had a stomach ache last night, cramping off and on. My back ached, my shoulder was aching, but I thought it was from hardly doing anything, and all the stress and fretting and worrying this week. I work hard, and Neil's made everything too easy. Maybe it was my fault." She couldn't look at Emily, wondering whether she'd think she was horrible, as well.

"Hey, you listen to me," Emily said. "Being pregnant is no picnic. I've been pregnant twice, and each time was different. Katie was hard, my first, and I was sick my entire pregnancy. Becky was easier, other than my back hurting off and on and being ridiculously tired. You ask Diana, too. She went into labor with her first while riding a horse, searching for Jed, and Christopher, he was overdue and she panicked over everything. So don't you dare blame yourself. That doctor shouldn't have said what he did. There are a lot of ifs, here. You already know you should have mentioned the spotting, but sometimes that's normal. How were you to know, Candy? Come on. Hindsight is always worth its weight in gold. None of us have a crystal ball. My Lord, I would have been a basket case this week if I were in your shoes. You handled it well. You did everything you could. It happened. It could have happened to Diana, me, even Laura, especially with our men." The way she said it helped a bit.

"What am I going to do, Emily?" she asked. She was worried, as she didn't know how to make Emily understand the distance Neil had put between them.

"Well, you're going to get some rest. You're going to get better. You and Neil can get married when you get out of here. You can stay at the ranch until you're well enough to travel. Enough worrying." Emily continued to rub her shoulder and then allowed her hand to slip away.

"I don't think there will be a wedding, Emily," Candy said. "I don't think you understand. It's different this time with Neil. I don't think he wants me anymore. He wants children, and I can't give him any now. I don't fit into his world. He'd be better off without me." She stiffened at the thought of losing Neil after everything she'd already lost. Emily pulled her hand away. "I'm tired, would you mind?" she said, refusing to look at Emily.

"Of course. I'll let you get some sleep. I'll come back later." Emily brushed Candy's back with her fingers and then pressed her hand to Candy's head. Then she left.

As soon as the door closed, Candy wept again.

Twenty~Five

Neil helped the caterer pack up the glasses, the crystal, the dishes. He carried, he lifted, he organized, and he moved stuff. He took down the decorations, set them in boxes, and put them out on the front deck faster than everything could be loaded into the vehicles. The food, mountains of it, had been moved into the kitchen, and someone else was putting it away. It could have been Laura, Diana, even Emily. Brad and Jed had offered to help, wanting him to talk, asking if he was okay until he finally barked, "Leave me alone!" Both had gestured in surrender and walked away.

Andy had watched him with that shrewd gaze from across the room, saying nothing. He'd stepped in when Neil was trying to take down one of the folding tables in the dining room and was having trouble finding the latch. He'd wanted to kick it and was about to when Andy reached down and flicked something bent on the metal leg. Andy then turned the table on its side and lifted one end, gesturing for him to do the other, and they had walked it outside together.

After the last item had been packed up and there was nothing left for him to do; that was when the whispers from his family became too much.

Rodney touched his shoulder and said, "Son, maybe you should take a break, sit down."

"I'm fine, Dad. I don't need to take a break or sit down. I need to do something," he snapped, which was something he never did with his father. They had a great relationship. Hell, he got along with everyone. He was always the reasonable one, except today.

"You're not fine. You're far from fine. Your girl is lying in a hospital bed after going through major surgery, and she's hurt, too, but instead of being there with her, you're here, snapping at everyone who's trying to help you," Rodney fired right back at him.

The kids were running around, but Becky stepped in and shooed them upstairs. Diana and Laura were holding their babies, watching Neil. Andy stood behind his wife, putting his hands on her shoulders, and he leaned down and whispered something in her ear. She nodded and then started upstairs behind Becky.

Emily frowned as she held one of the twins, swaying as she cuddled the baby. She started to say something before Brad gave her a meaningful look and said, "Don't, Emily."

"Well, maybe he needs to hear it," she said, not listening to her husband.

Brad, now back in jeans and a plaid shirt, put his hands on his hips. "Emily, this isn't the time." His tone was filled with warning.

"No, Brad, I'm sorry. Everyone is tiptoeing around Neil except Rodney, who is absolutely right. Neil, you should be with Candy. She didn't want you to leave. She's devastated—"

"Emily, that's enough!" Brad started toward his wife.

"No, Brad, it's not enough, and he's going to hear this!"

"Hear what, Emily? What are you talking about?" Neil snapped.

"Candy believes you blame her for what happened, as if any of that is her fault! Being pregnant is different for every woman. Our bodies are raging with hormones, changing, and what's normal for one woman isn't the same for another. How was she to know? She hadn't even seen a doctor yet, just found out she was pregnant with one of those home pregnancy tests; so how could you expect her to know something was wrong, with the amount of stress she was under? Neil, she believes you don't want her anymore, that you don't want to marry her because finding a woman to give you children is more important. I tried to tell her she was wrong, that when she gets out of the hospital you could still get married…" Emily stopped talking and stared at him. The confusion in her face turned into realization. "Oh my God, she's right."

He couldn't say anything. He loved Candy, but he needed to think, because he too had suffered a loss. Didn't they get that? "You've got it all figured out, don't you, Emily? She was spotting before the wedding, and she said nothing to anyone. She had symptoms, and I bet she told everyone she was fine," he snapped.

Brad jerked his gaze at Neil. "You watch how you talk to my wife," he said, voice full of warning.

"Oh, come on, Neil. I probably would have done the same thing in her shoes," Emily said. Brad blinked and glanced at his wife as she continued. "No, Neil, I don't have anything figured out. The only thing I do know is that there's a young woman who feels as if the entire world has abandoned her. You were her world, and she said you wouldn't even touch her. To suffer the kind of loss she did would tear me apart, especially when you can look back and see the signs you missed. But to have the one person she believed would always be there make her feel worse and then walk away? I don't think I could be as strong as she is right now. I don't know what to do for her, but I won't leave her alone." Emily turned to Brad and handed him Andy's baby. "I'm going back to the hospital," she said just as the steps creaked and Diana came back down.

"I'll go with you, Emily," Diana said, snuggling Christopher and then handing him to Jed. "Just let me pump some milk." She started for the back door, where a diaper bag was hanging, and pulled out a breast pump.

"Diana, you have a baby to nurse. You can't be taking off to the hospital," Jed said, holding his baby in one arm as he stalked toward his wife.

"You'll be just fine without me. So will Christopher. I'll leave you some milk in a bottle. You'll just need to heat it up."

Jed was in the kitchen now, obviously not happy, but Neil couldn't make out what he was saying to his wife. Apparently, she wasn't listening. Brad also appeared on edge and frustrated with Emily, and he slid his hand around her arm, uttering something in a low voice. He wasn't happy, and it was clear his caveman side was coming out as he tried telling Emily how it was going to be, but she wasn't listening. What she did do was slip on her coat, pat his arm, and take his truck keys from the hook. In less than ten minutes, Emily and Diana were driving Brad's truck down the driveway to be with Candy.

Twenty-Six

Neil shoved the pitchfork into the manure and shavings in the corner of the stall, dumping it into the wheelbarrow behind him. He swept the rest into the corner and scooped up more until the wheelbarrow was heaped. When he set the rake against the wall and hefted the wheelbarrow to steer it out of the stall, he caught Andy leaning against the door, watching him.

"Something on your mind, Andy?" he snapped. "Maybe you want to finish where Emily left off? I'm sure there's a piece of my hide still intact enough for you to have a go at it." He was being a first-class prick and he knew it, but it was the only way he could be right now. He wanted space, and it was pissing him off that no one would give him the room he needed to figure things out.

Andy didn't move, but he did hold out a beer. "Just thought you might like a beer, is all. There's enough liquor inside that Emily and Brad couldn't begin to make a dent in it, or it would turn them into alcoholics. Don't think it would be good for the kids."

Neil hesitated before yanking off the work gloves he'd

found in the tack room of the barn. He accepted the beer, took a swig, and let out a sigh. "Thank you."

Andy took a long swallow from the bottle but remained silent.

"So, do you plan on giving me a piece of your mind, telling me what an asshole I'm being and how I abandoned Candy when she needed me most?" Neil said.

Andy said nothing, just watched him with a heavy-lidded gaze and the best poker face Neil had ever seen.

"I didn't really mean what I said to her, but I can't understand how she didn't tell me she wasn't feeling well. She hides everything from me to the point that I have to figure it out. I don't know what the hell was going through her head. Who gives a shit who's going to be inconvenienced? I would have rather sat in a doctor's office and postpone the wedding. She has always been the most pig-headed, stubborn woman. I don't think I can keep doing this with her," he said, not realizing what he was deciding until he had put it into words and spoken it out loud.

He watched Andy for his reaction. He knew Brad and Jed would most likely have grabbed his shirtfront, slammed him against the barn wall, and done their best to talk some sense into him. Andy, though, didn't move. He took another swig of beer and glanced away as if gathering his thoughts.

"It's your life, Neil. Only you can make yourself happy. I can't tell you how to think, how to feel. I'm not your judge," Andy said, watching him.

Neil took another long swallow of beer. "Good. Thank you."

Andy nodded, watched Neil, and said, "The women are about ready to skin you alive, though, including your mother. It may be safer to stay out here for a bit."

"So why are you being so understanding? Why aren't

you like everyone else, trying to make me do the right thing? I mean, after all, aren't you the king of doing the right things?"

Andy offered a dry smile that wasn't amused. "I wouldn't know what the right thing is, Neil. I'm just like everyone else, trying to figure things out. Do you know what the right thing is for you and Candy?" Andy glanced away again as if to release the tension between them.

"No, not a clue. I just know I can't be there for her, the way I'm feeling. I'll hurt her more by what I'd like to say."

Andy just nodded. "Well, that's honest. You should know that Emily and Diana, even Brad and Jed, don't plan on letting you abandon her in the hospital. They'll look out for her if you need to take off. She'll be okay."

Neil shook his head. "That would make me quite the asshole, wouldn't it?" he asked, already knowing the answer.

"In some eyes, I suppose," Andy said.

"You've been mighty cryptic there, cos. Tell me about you and Laura. What are you doing now, since you spread your mighty wings and are no longer under your mother's thumb?"

Andy shot him a warning glance, worked his jaw, and finished off his beer. "I'm thinking of moving my family, Laura and the kids, out of the area. Head up to Montana, make a new start of things."

"Wow, seriously?" Neil studied his cousin and realized there was something more in the wind than Andy had shared. He knew something had happened, and Caroline must have pulled something pretty bad on Andy and Laura for him to move her and the children from the Friessen mansion. He just didn't know what it was, and with everything else going on, he had never asked. "You just bought a place, a small acreage, I heard. I never asked what happened to force your hand."

"Not the time, Neil. You've got a lot on your own plate, but sometimes family can be so poisonous and bad for you that it's best to cut ties and move away. No, Caroline always was a snake. Just never realized how dangerous she is, too. I'll make sure she never comes near my wife, my babies, even Gabriel." Andy swung his empty bottle between his fingers. "Besides, watching you and your family, Brad, Jed, Uncle Rodney, you'd never screw one of your own. I don't want my kids growing up with that. I think it's time to start a new era, scrape out a piece in another state where my family has no reach."

Now he knew what it was about Andy that was different. He hadn't been able to put his finger on it earlier. "I'm proud of you, Andy, for putting Laura and the kids first, walking away from everything your family has, the power, the wealth. In some ways, you're a lot like Jed. Hope it works out for you."

"So what are you going to do about Candy?" Andy asked.

"I don't know. With Candy, everything I did was with the intention of giving her a better life, showing her how much I love her. The problem is that I've always wanted her because she wouldn't give me the time of day. Do I love her enough to stay with her even if we have no children?"

"You can adopt, you know. I love Gabriel as if he were my own."

"Maybe you're a better man than I am, because I don't know if I could." Neil spat on the manure piled in the wheelbarrow. "Any more beer?"

Andy reached behind him and slid a box of a dozen over. He pulled out another, twisted off the top, and passed it to Neil. "Plenty. Kind of figured this is what you needed." Andy reached for another for himself, tipping his bottle forward to clink it with Neil's. "To the women we love and the hell they put us through."

Neil didn't say anything. As he watched his cousin drink, he wondered where he and Candy could fit in, whether it would even be possible for them to find a spot together with the rest of the Friessen men and the women they loved.

CHAPTER
Twenty~Seven

When Candy opened her eyes, the nurse was changing her IV bag, and she spotted Emily and Diana sitting in two chairs beside the bed. She lifted her head when a tiny thrill shot through her at the thought that maybe Neil was there too, but her heart sank as she dropped her head back on the pillow. He wasn't.

"Hey, you. How're you feeling?" Diana asked as she reached forward and touched Candy's leg.

"I'm stiff. I need to move," she said, her throat scratchy and dry. "Could I have some water?" She glanced at the nurse.

"Let's get you sitting up a bit, and we'll get you on your back. We need to get you up and walking, too." The nurse pushed the button on the bed until it moved up and she was almost sitting. Candy slid around onto her back, but when the nurse tried to take the pillow Candy held to her belly, she held tight.

"Please, I need the pillow," she said.

The nurse just nodded and walked away, and Diana

moved the rail down on the bed. She perched on the edge, her vibrant red hair tied back into a ponytail.

"I ache," Candy muttered just as the nurse walked back in, carrying a tray and setting it on the table. Diana stepped back, giving the nurse room to slide it over to Candy.

"I'll get you something for the pain. It's been a while since your last shot, and you're probably due. Here's some broth for you to sip, too. That's all you get after surgery. I'll be right back." The nurse slipped away again.

Candy reached for the cup of water, her hand trembling.

"Here, let me get it for you." Diana reached for the cup and held the straw to Candy's lips.

She took a sip and stopped when she felt a pull deep inside her, where she'd been ripped apart in surgery, where they had taken out her womb and ovaries and left her barren. She waved the cup away and leaned back, and Diana started fussing, plumping her pillow, smoothing the covers, and lifting the lid on the bowl of soup just as the nurse walked back in.

"Eat what you can, honey. You need your strength," the nurse said. She injected something into Candy's IV bag and then left again.

Diana put a spoon in the bowl and then set a napkin on Candy's chest, tucking it into the top of her hospital gown.

"You're not going to feed me too, are you?" Candy asked.

Diana smiled down at her as she edged closer. "Only if you need me to."

"You may as well let her," Emily muttered. "It would make her happy, having someone to mother."

Candy allowed Diana to spoon some of the broth into

her mouth. She choked and then coughed. "Oh, that hurts." She pressed the pillow to her abdomen.

Diana slid the table away. "Let's get you sitting up a little more," she said, moving the bed a little higher and then sliding the table back. This time, Candy took the spoon and tried a smaller mouthful of the extremely awful, bland broth.

"This is disgusting," she said.

"I'll bring you something from home tomorrow—" Emily started.

"You mean if Brad lets you come tomorrow. I thought he was going to order you upstairs," Diana said.

"He just didn't want to have to look after the kids, but it wasn't as if he had to cook anything. There's enough food left behind from the caterer that I don't know what we'll do with all of it."

"I'm sorry to have caused any trouble," Candy said. She worried about the commotion, with everything back at Emily and Brad's and all the family still there. There was nothing she could do.

"Oh, stop it. You've apologized enough," Diana said, sitting at the foot of the bed. "None of this was your fault. Everyone should be apologizing to you, if that would make you feel better, but it won't help, because what happened was out of your control. You didn't plan this."

"I don't know. I should have said something, and I didn't. Neil blames me." She sighed and pushed away the tray. "I guess it's good that it happened when it did, before we were married. This way is easier. Less messy."

Both women exchanged a look, their expressions grim. "It's not good that it happened at all, Candy, but it happened just the same, and you and Neil will move past this. You'll be fine, you'll get married, and…"

"We won't have children," Candy said, interrupting

Diana.

"Candy, you can adopt. There are so many children who need the good home that you and Neil could give them." Emily didn't get up, but she leaned forward, trying to get her point across.

"Adopting isn't as easy as you think, Emily," Candy said. "Besides, maybe I'm not cut out to be a mother. Maybe this is the universe's way of telling me that. I mean, let's face it, I was scared around your children, terrified you'd ask me to hold your baby, Diana. Besides, Neil can't stand to be in the same room with me. He's probably trying to figure out a way to break it off with me. He wants children. Have you seen him with yours? You didn't see the starry-eyed look he had when he found out I was pregnant. I could tell he'd already made plans for the baby, a name, which little league team the kid would play on—Neil would have coached it, too."

"Come on, Candy. That's not fair. Neil loves you. I may want to have words with him and tell him what a lout he is for deserting you now, but he's hurting, too. He's not okay. He's not okay at all," Emily said.

"Maybe so, but you and I both know the kind of circles Neil moves in. He'd be better off with someone comfortable with that kind of power, with the schmoozing. He needs a polished princess who wants to stay home and give him a dozen babies, but that's not me. Let's be realistic—I don't belong in his world." She turned her head away. "I don't want to talk about this anymore." She could feel a warmth running through her body as the pain medication took effect. Her eyelids felt heavy, and as she blinked and turned her head, watching two women she barely knew who were determined to sit vigil with her; Candy suddenly mourned the loss of her two new sisters, a loss that added to the ache of losing Neil.

"Wake up!" a deep voice boomed, and Neil pressed his hands to his throbbing temples.

A foot kicked his leg, and he immediately felt the straw bale poking into his back. He sat up, his head feeling as if it were a football someone had kicked around. He rested his head in his hand and took a whiff of stale beer mixed with manure. He was still in the barn, and a horse blanket had been tossed over him. Neil blinked, and there was his big brother Brad glowering down on him.

"Did you solve anything by getting shitfaced?" he asked.

Neil blinked and rested his elbows on his knees as he sat up. He looked around for Andy but didn't see him, though he did spot the empty bottle of whiskey they'd also shared.

"What do you want, Brad?" he groaned.

"I want you to get up and go take care of your woman so Jed and I can get ours back," Brad snapped.

Neil leaned back against the barn wall. "They didn't come home last night?"

"Diana popped in for an hour to pump some more milk. She and Jed got into it pretty good. Dad and Mom had to drive Laura, the kids, and Andy back to the hotel, as Andy was pretty wasted. Mom's not impressed, by the way."

"Well, you know what? I have no control over anything Diana and Emily do. They're your wives. You deal with them," Neil said, and before his brain could even absorb what a stupid remark he had made, Brad had grabbed him by the shirtfront and yanked him up.

"What is wrong with you?" he snapped. He let Neil go and kicked the empty bottle on the barn floor, his gaze taking in the empty beer bottles scattered there, too. "Neil, I've been patient with you, and so has Jed. Andy, obviously, was more interested in helping you tie one on than getting you to go make things right with Candy. It should be you sitting beside her hospital bed. I don't know what you're thinking, but you're hurting her. Or is that what you're trying to do—send her the message that she's no use to you now that she can't have kids anymore and that's all she was good for, that you don't love her enough? That's pretty low, especially for you. I've never known you to treat a woman this way."

"Look, I feel bad. Andy is the only one who's given me space to think. He hasn't come down on me. He's listened, because I don't know what the hell to do. I didn't expect this, and I can't help the way I feel. I want children; my own kids. Do you get that?" he shouted. He had to hold onto his head, which was pounding harder, as if it would explode from his outburst.

"Look, I know you do. We all know, and I don't know how I would feel if I were in your shoes, but if that was

Emily this had happened to—I'd be glued to her bedside. I'd be with her, worried about her." Brad put his hand on Neil's shoulder. "If having kids is more important to you than Candy, you need to let her know, but kicking her when she's down is not the way to do it. You need to go to the hospital, take care of her. After she's on her feet, you need to let her down gently. She's a nice lady, Neil. If you walk away from her now, Emily and I will look out for her, but I don't think Emily will ever forgive you, and I don't want that kind of rift in the family. Decide now; what kind of man are you?" Brad started to leave before turning back to Neil. "Oh, and clean up this mess. Get these bottles out of my barn. I have a ranch to run, and in about an hour I've got the farrier coming to shoe some horses," he said. Then he left.

Neil slumped onto the hay bale with one hell of a hangover. He wanted to kick something because he knew Brad was right. How was he going to face Candy? She'd know how he was feeling: hurt, angry, and confused. Hell, he didn't know what he wanted out of this mess, but what he did know was that he needed to suck it up, go see his girl, and figure out where they would go from here.

Neil still felt as if something had crawled inside him and died, but at least the pounding in his head had dimmed to something he could live with after swallowing a couple Advil. He'd cleaned up the barn, showered to remove the stench of old whiskey that seeped from his pores, and grabbed some of the leftovers stuffed in the fridge from the wedding feast. There were deviled eggs, and he'd used some of the roast beef to make a sandwich.

The kids were fussy, and with Jed and Brad the only two home to look after them, the house had quickly become a disaster. The kitchen was scattered with dirty dishes, leftover food on plates, and the kitchen table still held the remnants of the kids' breakfast. Brad and Jed appeared cranky and ready to snap, and while Neil pulled on his black leather coat, Jed held a fussing Christopher and tossed him his truck keys.

"Take my truck, and send my wife back here," he snapped. Neil was pretty sure Jed hadn't slept much. He appeared tired, and when Danny started fussing and pulling on his jeans, he let out a sigh. "Come on, Danny. Give Daddy a break."

"Daddy, up," Danny whined, holding out his arms. Jed gazed at the ceiling as Christopher fussed more and more, winding up to let out a wail.

Brad had Becky in his arms, her face smeared with peanut butter, still in her pajamas. "Come on, Danny. Let your daddy feed Christopher."

One kid started crying, "Where's Mommy?" Soon, this changed to "I want Mommy!" and Neil knew he had better do something quick.

"I'm leaving for the hospital. Hey, Danny, bud, I'll send your mommy home," Neil said, rubbing the top of Danny's head and running out the door as Christopher started crying.

At the hospital, the elevator doors dinged and opened to the second-floor ward. Neil stepped out and took in the nurses and doctors, the visitors walking the halls. He took a deep breath as he started walking. Each step closer did little to comfort him. In fact, the closer he got, the more he dreaded seeing Candy. He had handled all of this badly. He shouldn't have left Candy—he knew that now. He didn't know what he wanted, but as he stepped closer to her room and felt the enormous gulf between them, which had been put there by him, he realized there was only so much he could blame on their circumstances.

He hesitated, giving himself a quick pep talk, before pushing the door open and stopping when three pairs of eyes glared back at him.

Thirty

When Candy saw Neil open the door to her room, her heart instantly started thudding against her ribcage. Her breath caught, and she didn't miss how the air had thickened with electricity in the few seconds that Neil had stood watching them. He raised his eyebrows, and Candy noticed how bloodshot his eyes were.

Diana had been brushing Candy's long, dark hair, which was damp from the shower she'd just taken. She was so tired from that small effort of walking the hall and standing in the shower that it had taken everything she had to walk back to the room and climb into bed.

Diana and Emily had stayed all night. The nurse had brought them each a blanket and pillow, and they'd slept upright in those padded chairs. It didn't look comfortable, and before falling asleep, Candy had asked them to go home. Diana had gone for a few hours to feed her baby and pump some milk, but other than that, they hadn't left her side.

Candy was touched by their support and their refusal

to desert her. They said she was family, and family stuck with you and had your back, especially when life decided to smack you upside the back of the head. She appreciated that and felt closer to both of these wonderful ladies than she could have ever hoped for.

Neil took all three of them in with his shrewd gaze, and appeared to pull into himself even more; she noticed how pale he looked, and then started to worry about him. He shoved his hands in his pockets and didn't move any closer to her, staying by the door. *Well, here we go,* she thought. With this awkwardness, maybe her knight in shining armor wasn't so knightly after all. He was human and flawed, and he couldn't handle her situation, so she said nothing.

"Good morning, Neil," Emily said from the chair. The cushion creaked when she slid around to have a better look. "Hmm, you look like crap."

Neil looked ready to snarl. "Your husbands want you home," he said, though he immediately realized that probably wasn't the best way to start, as the air between him and Emily appeared to snap. "I'm here now, so you two should go before the house falls apart. Brad and Jed are pretty close to losing it, and the kids are asking for you two."

Well, that did it. Both women perked up like lionesses protecting their young. "Are the kids okay? What's going on at home?" Emily asked, sounding a little worried as she slid forward, exchanging a look with Diana.

"Your husbands are drowning, and they'll be the first to admit they can't do it all. They don't want your job. They love the kids, but they don't want to play mommy for one more minute. Your kids are done with their daddies. They want you."

"Candy, I need to go save my kids," Emily said. She stood up, dumping the blanket in a heap on the chair.

Emily's face was tired and pale, and her hair was a rumpled mess. She tidied it with her fingers as Diana scooped her jacket up from the chair and shrugged it on.

"We'll come back after we get the kids squared away," she said, patting Candy's leg and leaning forward to hug her tight. She glanced at Neil. "Will you be okay with him?"

Diana made her feel so good—Emily, too. She was sure the women would toss Neil out on her say-so. "No, we're fine," she said. "Go be with your kids and your husbands. Don't worry about coming back. Look after your kids first. I'm going to sleep most of the day, anyway."

"You call us if you need anything," Emily said.

The door popped open, and the doctor strode in with Candy's chart. Diana and Emily slipped out the door with a wave, and Neil allowed his gaze to drift away from Candy to the doctor. The doctor paused and shook his hand.

"Neil Friessen," Neil said.

"Ah, yes, sorry. Candy's husband, right?" the doctor said as he glanced at the chart, setting it on the sliding table.

"No, we're not married," Candy muttered before Neil could say it. She didn't think she could listen to him say it without her heart breaking in two.

Neil firmed his lips, obviously annoyed, but he didn't look at her. "We were getting married when Candy collapsed, so technically we're not married."

"Ah, I see. Well, I just want to take a look at the incision, see how you're healing up." The doctor slid the covers back and lifted her gown. Candy couldn't look, so she turned her head toward the window, where she didn't have to look at Neil. She felt the pull of the bandage and the doctor poking around. He hit an especially sore spot, and she let out a hiss.

"Sore?" he asked. "It looks a little inflamed around the staples. That's to be expected. I have to say you're doing remarkably well, considering we had to remove not just both fallopian tubes but your entire uterus."

Candy never answered him.

"Well, I see no reason why we can't release you tomorrow. Your temperature looks good, and your vitals. We'll get some more blood work today, and if everything checks out, we can let you go home first thing tomorrow." The doctor clicked his pen, tucking it into the pocket of his white coat. Candy pulled her gown down and slid the blanket up and over her shoulders, tucking it under her chin. She noticed Neil hadn't missed her need to hide from him.

"Thank you, Doctor." Neil shook the man's hand again, and the doctor patted Neil's shoulder as if they were best buds before slipping out of the room.

Candy looked at the door. Neil didn't move any closer, pulling the chair that Emily had been sitting on back so that it was about four feet from her bed. There was no way he could touch her. He sat down, set his ankle over his knee, and clasped his hands. She stared at those large hands, remembering all too well how they felt skimming over her bare skin, exploring every part of her. She mourned the loss and swallowed the lump in her throat.

"Did you sleep well last night?" he asked.

So they were being polite. "Yes," she said, flicking her gaze to the awkwardness in his expression. He glanced away. "You didn't have to come," she said, waiting for him to respond.

He let out a mournful laugh that was anything but

happy. "Oh, yes, I did. If I didn't send Emily and Diana home, Brad and Jed were going to string me up."

She nodded. The lump in her throat expanded in her chest until it burned. "Well, you can tell them you came. Tell Emily and Diana they don't have to come back."

He nodded and then cleared his throat roughly. "I'm sorry if I hurt you."

She met the sorrow in his gaze, and she had to look away before she teared up again. "I know," she said. She squeezed her pillow and then pushed the button to raise the bed as she lay on her side.

"We should talk about tomorrow," he said. "I'll pick you up in the morning when you're going to be released. You can stay at Emily and Brad's for a few days until you get the go-ahead to travel. Then I'll book a flight home." He rubbed his chin and then gestured with his hand as if arranging a business deal, so unemotional. She just watched him, wondering how it had come to this. She wished he'd go, but, at the same time, she prayed the real Neil would show up and tell her this was all a big joke.

"I'm kind of tired. You don't have to stay," she said. She didn't look at him, praying that this time he'd get mad and refuse to leave, that he would demand to be there for her. Instead, she heard the chair legs scrape back, and she felt him lean over and hesitate before giving her a peck on the side of her head. It felt cold and dutiful. She squeezed her eyes shut, held her breath, and waited until she knew he was gone. Then it hit her as she replayed what he'd said; her, just her alone, staying at Emily and Brad's, and flying home. Not once had he said "we." Well, at least she knew without a doubt that this had been his subtle way of saying they were done. He really wasn't all that different from the average guy out there. He, too, played that game; take the hint and get lost.

The knowledge certainly didn't make it hurt any less, but she had her pride. She wouldn't ask him for anything, and she couldn't rely on his family. Candy needed to get back on the horse, in a manner of speaking, and take care of things herself. But how? She stared at the telephone beside the bed as a thought came to her.

She reached for the receiver, closing her eyes for a second as she thought of the number, and then pressed zero, waiting for the hospital operator to come on. "I'd like to make a long-distance call," she said.

The operator hesitated and asked her if she had a calling card. Before Candy could say that she didn't, the operator realized what room she was in and said it was no problem. Candy realized it had to be Neil's money paying for all this. She rattled off the number, and the operator placed the call.

It took a minute, and then it rang two, three times before she heard the deep, scratchy voice of an older woman who had been her banker and was someone she thought of as a friend. Stella, a vibrant redhead in her seventies, had a past and a wardrobe any woman would envy.

"Stella, it's Candy," she said.

There was a hesitation for a second before Stella said, "Well, hello, Missus Friessen! How does it feel, being the wife of the most eligible man in this part of the country?" She let out her trademark laugh, which always put a smile on Candy's face—but not today.

"We're not married," she said, and she heard a gasp on the other end.

"Why not? What happened, Candy?" Stella asked, sounding suddenly suspicious.

"I'm in the hospital. I, uh…" Her throat closed up, and

she couldn't find the words to explain to Stella how wrong things had gone.

"What? Where's Neil? Are you okay?" Stella, who never appeared ruffled by anything, sounded frantic on the other end.

"I was pregnant. It turned out it was ectopic, it ruptured, and they did a hysterectomy. Neil's gone. It's over between us." She squeezed out a tear and then wiped her face, listening to silence on the other end.

"Oh, Candy, I am so sorry, honey. For you to have to go through something like this isn't fair. Where's Neil? I don't understand how he's gone. This doesn't make any sense."

"It was too much for him, Stella. He wants children. I can't give them to him. I wouldn't have fit into his world anyway. It's best this way," she said again, wondering when she'd really believe it. "They're releasing me from the hospital tomorrow. I don't have any money, Stella. I didn't know who else to call. After the storm, I let Neil handle everything. I know my property's gone, but I was wondering if you knew who bought it and if they'd consider renting it to me."

She could hear Stella groaning in the background. Maybe she was trying to find a way to let her down easy. "Candy, honey, yeah… about that. Have you talked to Neil about the property?" Stella asked in an odd way.

"No, we haven't talked about it at all. He just told me not to worry about anything, that he'd take care of me," Candy said, remembering all too well during the storm, and afterward, how protective Neil had been of her. For the first time ever, she had felt cherished. "Look, Stella, I know the answer is probably no, but did you sell my property?"

"Candy, that was out of my hands. The bank fore-closed. The property was bought."

"Was there any money or anything left for me?"

She sighed on the other end. "Candy, I'm sorry. There was nothing for you. With the back taxes, the mortgage… the investor paid off everything that was owing. There was nothing extra."

"I see. Well, would this investor be willing to rent a piece of it to me?" she said. She couldn't believe she was asking, since she didn't have a dime to pay any amount of rent, but she'd work it out when she got home. She'd find a job. She would do anything.

"Candy, I really think you need to talk to Neil," Stella said again.

Why did she keep harping on that? "Neil's gone, Stella. He made it clear that we're done, and I'd just as soon not talk to him again. I need to buy a plane ticket home. Would I be able to borrow the airfare? You know I'll find a way to pay it back."

"I'll buy your ticket. Don't you worry about paying it back. But listen, Candy. That property of yours has got nothing on it. Even if you rented a piece of it, where would you live, in a tent?" she barked on the other end.

"Maybe I could talk to the buyer. We could work something out. I could help clear the land. I know it was a mess from the hurricane. I can help sift through and be part of the cleanup. Was it someone local who bought it? Maybe I could talk to them."

There was hesitation on the other end, and she could hear Stella tapping a pen on her desk and clicking her tongue. "I didn't want this to come from me," she said.

"What are you talking about, Stella?"

"Neil."

"What about Neil?" she asked again, wondering if she'd suddenly become dimwitted.

"Candy, Neil is the investor who bought your property. He said he was going to tell you."

If someone had sucker punched her in the gut, right where her incision was, it wouldn't have hurt as much as what Stella had just said. Maybe she had misunderstood— maybe she hadn't heard right?

"Stella, are you telling me Neil bought my property?" she asked in a voice that was almost lifeless to her own ears.

"I'm sorry, honey. I didn't want you to find out this way. I thought Neil would have told you by now." She paused. "Do you still want a plane ticket home?"

"Yes," Candy said.

Stella said she'd take care of the details and apologized to her again before she hung up. Candy stared at the closed door to her room, and for a minute she wondered whether anyone would notice if she slipped away now. Probably not. She had no family, no money, and no home.

Thirty-One

"What do you mean, she's gone?" Neil said. He stared at the freshly made, empty, hospital bed, which was waiting for another patient. Candy was supposed to have been released that morning.

He hadn't gone right home to Emily and Brad's after leaving the night before. He had driven around for hours, pulling into their driveway just before dinnertime. He had been greeted by icy glares from Emily, Diana, and his mother. Rodney had seemed distant but asked him how Candy was doing, and he had replied that she was fine, letting them believe he'd spent the entire time he'd been gone at Candy's bedside. Andy and Laura were there, too, but only to say goodbye, as they were driving home at first light. Andy and Neil had exchanged a hug, and then Neil had disappeared upstairs to his bedroom.

Now, as he stood in the doorway, wondering what the hell he had missed, Emily appeared beside him.

"Where's Candy?" she asked, holding a bouquet of flowers and staring at the empty room.

"The nurse just said she's gone. She's already been released."

Emily's expression filled with alarm. "Where is she?"

Neil started toward the nurses station. "Excuse me," he said to one of the nurses in blue scrubs at the desk.

"Yes, can I help you?" She glanced up at him.

"I was just told that my…" he cleared his throat, "that Candy McCrae was released. We're here to pick her up, and she's not in her room. She had an emergency hysterectomy. I'm confused. Is she waiting somewhere?" He looked around behind him and back at the nurse.

Another nurse leaned down and whispered something to the first, who typed something into the computer. "She was released last night," she said.

"What?" Emily said. "Where did she go?"

"Don't know," the nurse said. "Excuse me." She grabbed a handful of charts and walked away. Neil spotted the doctor as he approached the desk.

"Mister Friessen, what can I do for you?" he asked.

"We came to pick up Candy, but we just found out that she was released last night. No one called us to come pick her up," Neil said. An awful worry had started to prickle the back of his neck.

Emily chimed in, saying, "She has no clothes here. I brought something for her to wear." She showed the doctor the bag she carried. "What could she be wearing?"

The doctor frowned and then called one of the nurses over. "Did someone pick Candy McCrae up last night?"

The nurse glanced at Neil and then back at the doctor. "No, she took a cab, told me she had no one coming for her."

"I don't believe this. What is she wearing, a hospital gown—and wandering the streets?" Neil barked.

"We loaned her some scrubs," said the nurse before walking away.

The doctor shook his head. "I'm sorry." He shrugged, flipping through her chart. "I don't know what to tell you. I see it was the doctor on call last night who released her early. Very odd. The only thing I can suggest is to check with security downstairs to see if they know the cab she took."

The doctor was then called away, and Neil could feel Emily's gaze burning into him.

"What happened when you were here yesterday?" she snapped. "Obviously it didn't go well, so tell me again how she's 'fine.' She took a cab in her condition?" She was getting a little loud, so Neil guided her to the elevator. He jabbed the button and stepped inside, and she followed like a cat stalking its prey.

"She said she was tired," Neil tried to explain.

"Were you or weren't you here with her for the four hours you were gone?" she asked in a determined voice Neil had heard her use a time or two on Brad.

Neil shut his eyes. "No."

"Oh, Neil, what is going on with you?"

She touched his arm, and he wanted to weep as he stared at her and shook his head when he couldn't get a word out.

"Neil, does she have any money?" she asked.

He shook his head again.

"We have to find her," Emily said.

They stepped out of the elevator, and Neil stopped and stared at the front door as a cab pulled up. "I have an idea," he said as he jogged to the front door, waving at the cabby just as an older man opened the back door and started to climb in.

"Excuse me, sir, but this is my cab," the man said.

"It's all yours. I just need to ask the driver a question." Neil opened the front door and leaned in as the cabby stared from Neil to the older man in back. "There was a woman who took a cab last night from the hospital," he said to the cabby.

"Sir, I wasn't working last night. You'd want to talk to dispatch, but there are two cab companies in this town," the man said.

Neil knew the man wasn't going to be any more help, so he thanked him and shut the door, watching as the cab drove away. Emily was standing behind him, wide eyed, and seemed to say with her hands, *What's next?*

Neil started walking inside, extending his hand to turn Emily and guide her back in. "Let's find out who called her the cab," he said. He stopped at the front desk, where a chunky older woman with short curly hair was sitting.

She glanced up as they approached. "Can I help you?"

"Yes, my fiancée was released early last night, and apparently she took a cab. We're trying to find out where she went and which cab was called for her," Neil said, hoping it didn't sound as strange as he thought it had, coming from his own mouth.

The woman acted as if she'd heard it before and asked the name of the patient. She typed something on her keyboard and said, "There's a problem, sir. We didn't get the settlement of her hospital bill, and there was a long-distance charge on there, as well. Will you be settling the account?"

Who would she call? raced through his mind as he fumbled for his wallet. "I already filled out the forms. I had medical insurance for Candy. It's under my name." He slid the medical card across the counter to the woman.

She typed in the numbers and then printed something

off. "The insurance didn't cover everything. This is the balance due." She set a printout in front of him.

Neil pulled out his credit card and handed it to her, and then he asked, "Excuse me. Can I see the number she called?"

The woman pointed with her pen to the bottom of the page, which showed the long-distance phone charge and the phone number.

Neil looked at the number and then shut his eyes. "Oh, shit."

"What is it, Neil?" Emily asked as he stared at the number again.

"That would be my banker, a friend of mine, Stella," Neil said.

Emily appeared confused and asked, "Why would Candy call her?"

"To try to get money—and because she doesn't have anyone else," Neil said just as the woman came back with his credit card and receipt.

He pulled his cell phone out, opened the phone book, and dialed Stella's number. She answered on the second ring.

"Well, hello, Neil." She sounded frosty and cold, as if she had a bone to pick with him.

"Stella, did Candy call you last night?" he asked as he stepped away from the desk and into the middle of the lobby.

"She did. Quite the story, too. Seriously, Neil, I don't understand how you could hurt her like that. Do you have any idea what a woman goes through after a hysterectomy? It's even worse at Candy's age. My God, she's a young woman, Neil. Her life is just beginning, and because she can't give you a child, you throw her to the curb and let her know she's of no use to you anymore? Neil, I've always liked you. We were friends, but I never in a million years pinned you as the same type of dirty dog as Candy's father, old Randy McCrae. Look at the mess and the debt he left her! She trusted you, Neil, and you broke her heart." Stella sighed on the other end.

"That's not how it was at my end. She hurt me, and she scared the hell out of me. I may have not handled it right—"

Stella cut him off, yelling through the phone. "Did you end things with her and tell her you were done with her, that she was of no use to you anymore?"

"No, I didn't say that," Neil spat out.

"Then why does she think that?" Stella snapped.

"Because I'm a bastard," he snapped. "I couldn't be honest with her because I was too angry with her, so instead I stayed away because I didn't want to hurt her. I needed to figure out what I wanted out of this mess."

Emily was standing in front of him, gesturing, trying to figure out what was going on. Neil pulled the cell phone from his mouth and started to say something before shaking his head. He felt as if his world had splintered into a million pieces, and it couldn't get any worse.

"By the way, Neil, she kept asking about her property."

Okay, he was wrong. It could get worse, much worse, as an icy dread slithered down his back. He had a sick feeling that all of his choices had been made for him. "What did you say to her?" he growled.

Emily looked around to see if anyone had noticed. Neil didn't care and started walking toward the door.

"She kept pushing, Neil. She wanted to rent a piece of the property. She asked who bought it. She wanted to talk to them, and then she wanted to be part of the cleanup crew. Neil, she had major surgery, and she was all prepared to work herself to the bone," Stella added.

"Stella, what did you tell her?" he asked again, the warning clear.

She sighed before saying, "I'm sorry, Neil. I didn't know what else to say, so I told her that you bought it."

This time, Neil pulled the phone from his ear as he pressed his hand to his head.

Emily touched his arm. "Neil, what's going on?"

He wanted to weep, and he had to clear his throat so he could speak. "Where is she, Stella? She has no money. We just found out she borrowed a pair of scrubs to leave the hospital. She has no clothes, not even a coat. She just had major surgery."

"I arranged for a plane ticket home. She took that small commuter plane last night to Seattle. She's on the morning flight home. It leaves in an hour," Stella answered.

"I don't understand," he started.

"I paid for everything, Neil. I took care of her arrangements, the cab, the flight, even her hotel. I sent some cash so she could buy some food, some clothes, whatever she needed. I'll pick her up when she gets home."

"Stella, I have to talk to her. She won't understand why I bought it, and she's going to think the worst."

"Well, of course she is. You should have told her already. You told me you would. It was only a matter of time before she found out."

Neil started walking in circles, thinking, trying to figure out how to stop Candy. "Stella, I need your help. I have to talk to her. I need time to get to Seattle. I need to make her understand why I bought it."

"Neil, unless you have some magical way of getting to Seattle before her plane leaves in an hour, I don't see what I can do to help. The ticket's waiting for her, and there's nothing I can do to stop it."

He was thinking, and he realized in that second that she couldn't go anywhere. "She doesn't have her passport," he said.

Stella said, "They won't let her on the plane. What are you going to do, Neil?"

"I'm going to go get her," he said as he grabbed Emily's arm and hurried her to the truck with him.

"Well, how are you going to make her go with you? If you recall, Neil, Candy can go nose to nose with you when she wants, and I'm pretty sure she won't let you touch her," Stella said.

"Well, I don't plan on giving her a choice."

"So does this mean you've figured out what you want where Candy is concerned?"

Neil opened Emily's door and gestured her inside. "Yes. Oh, Stella, try paging her at the airport so she doesn't take off when she finds out she can't get on the plane. Make sure she stays put."

"Well, what am I supposed to tell her?" she asked, sounding a little annoyed.

"Stella, you can think on your feet faster than anyone else I know. You'll come up with something." Neil hung up and slid behind the wheel. Emily was shaking her head, and he could feel her eyes on him as he backed out. "Call your husband. We're going to Seattle," Neil said, tossing Emily his cell phone as he backed out of the stall.

"Seattle? Are we driving? That will take hours," Emily sputtered.

"No choice, Emily. There are two flights a day to Seattle—six in the morning and seven at night. Besides, it takes two and a half hours at the speed limit. Should be able to shave a fair bit off that," Neil said. He saw her worry, but she nodded and called Brad.

Thirty~Two

How do you begin to explain to someone how you feel when you don't understand yourself? Neil had been driving almost an hour in relative silence with Emily. He knew she was trying to absorb what he'd shared, the reason why Candy had left the hospital, but what she hadn't asked was why he had deserted Candy to begin with.

"Emily, I'm not a bad person," he said.

She rustled in her seat and sighed. "I know that, Neil."

"Do you know what it was like with Candy during the storm? Even before that, I had always wanted her." He glanced across the open space of the truck to Emily, who was watching him, listening to what he had to say.

"She would cross the street to get away from me, give me that 'Eat shit and die' look, but that was because that worthless father of hers had messed with her head. It was always about that piece of land her father owned. Yes, I wanted it. Did you know that her father offered her to me for a price in exchange for that property?"

Emily appeared shocked, and her eyes widened.

"He wanted to be linked with the Friessen name, but there was no way Dad and I would allow that; not with the shady things we were pretty sure he was into."

"Did Candy know?" Emily asked.

"Not until later. She thought her dad walked on water. He was all she had, but he drank himself to death, letting her believe I was responsible for their plight."

"Why would she think that?" Emily asked.

"Because he told her so, and he warned me he would make sure she'd never have anything to do with me, not ever, if I refused to give him what he wanted. That old bastard did it, too." Neil would have spit on his grave if he could. All of Candy's worries, her fear, and her insecurity in standing up for herself, he knew her father had done that to her.

"That's horrible, Neil."

"I knew she was drowning in bills. She was going to lose her place, but she wouldn't take anything from me. She'd go to the devil himself before coming to me. When the storm hit, it was Stella who called me, told me to go and get her, that she wouldn't leave her property. The hurricane was heading right for us, and I didn't think she was reckless enough to stay, but I was wrong. My heart damn near stopped when I drove in there and saw her beat-up old truck still parked in front of the house. When I finally found her, pinned down and injured… Well, you already know we didn't get out in time," he finished. Just thinking about it again had his stomach in knots.

"Brad and I worried about you during that storm. When we found out you didn't make it out before it hit, Brad was on the phone with anyone he could call for information: shelters, hospitals, the Red Cross. The TV was on constantly as he waited for updates, trying to find out whether you were okay. He was about to head down there to find you himself," Emily said.

"I didn't know that," Neil said, touched that his brother would have done that.

"He loves you, Neil."

He had to clear his throat. He loved his brothers, both of them. His family was so important to him, even though he was sure Brad was ready to kick his ass across the county.

"So tell me, Neil, why did you turn your back on Candy?" Emily asked. It was the one question he'd been asking himself over and over.

"I felt betrayed," he said.

"What?" Emily said in disbelief.

"It's a matter of trust, Emily. I know it was a rough week, but it's always been something. She's always holding something back, and I thought we had finally gotten to a place where she could talk to me. When I heard of the symptoms, that she had been spotting and said nothing to me—I was hurt because she didn't trust me enough to tell me."

"Oh, Neil, it's not as simple as that," Emily said. "Sometimes when you have such thick walls up to protect your heart, it isn't just a matter of trusting and sharing. She has to know that you'll be patient enough that no matter how hard she pushes or hides, you'll be there and you won't go anywhere. Then she'll let the walls down and trust you completely. But you just showed her that she was right," Emily said, her voice calm.

"How did I do that?" Neil asked.

"You weren't there for her," she replied.

"I didn't want to hurt her. That's why I wasn't there. I didn't know what I would say to her. I wanted to shake her, to yell at her," Neil said, wondering why Emily couldn't get that.

"You hurt her by not being there. You should have stayed. You should have gotten mad at her, told her how hurt you were that she wouldn't say anything. You should have told her that even though you were furious, you weren't leaving," Emily said. "You want children, Neil, badly. She knows that—we all do, but you shouldn't have let her think she was of no use to you, that children were more important."

"Emily, that's not fair. I didn't know what I felt, but when I heard that doctor say 'hysterectomy,' the idea of not having children… My dreams had just been shattered. Yes, I want children, my own children, and when someone suddenly takes something so real from you, it sucker punches you. It took everything I had just to breathe. I blamed her, you're right, but I didn't want to hurt her, too." He stopped talking and rested his elbow on the edge of the door.

"Neil, do you still want to marry Candy, even though she can't have kids?"

He knew she was waiting for an answer, but he couldn't answer her because, in his own mind, he still hadn't been able to separate Candy from the children he wanted. He flicked the signal light on the truck and passed another vehicle as they approached the freeway into Seattle.

"Neil, you're going to have to figure out what to say to Candy. You have to understand that she may not want to come with you," Emily added when he didn't answer her.

"I know. I just don't have a clue what to say. If this were a business deal, I'd charm her." He smiled at Emily, but she frowned in return.

"Can I give you some advice, Neil?"

"Am I going to want to hear this?" he replied.

"Neil, just speak from the heart. Tell her how you really feel about everything," Emily said.

"What if she won't listen? I mean, she knows I bought her property, and me not telling her is——"

"Exactly what she did to you when she asked me to help her get a pregnancy test without sharing her suspicions with you."

Neil did a double take, surprised. "Uh, I don't know what to say. I didn't think you would get it."

"Neil, I want you both to be happy. I don't want to see either of you hurt——"

Neil's cell phone rang, interrupting Emily. He grabbed it with his free hand, noticing the long-distance number. "Stella, what's going on? I'm almost there."

"Well, you better hurry. That girl is freaking out. I just got off the phone with her again. She's waiting at the ticket counter for her new passport to arrive from the consulate."

"Wait a second. How is the consulate able to send a passport just like that?" Neil snapped.

"They're not," Stella barked. "I lied, but she doesn't know that. The girl believes I can perform miracles, so you better not blow this, or that girl will never trust anyone again."

"Got it. I'll figure something out. I'll call you after I've found her."

Neil hung up and tossed the phone on the seat, pressing the gas and moving into the fast lane.

"Neil?" Emily asked, setting her hand on the dashboard as he sped up.

"Just hang on. Candy is still at the airport, waiting for a passport that will never arrive. I just don't know what shape she's going to be in when we get there."

"Then we better hurry," Emily said just as a siren and lights flashed behind them.

"Oh, shit," Neil said as he spotted the police cruiser behind him. He slowed and pulled over, rolling down his window as the cop approached.

"Any idea how fast you were going?" the cop asked.

"Sorry, Officer. My girl is at the airport, and she's hurt…"

"Save it. License and registration, please," the cop said, cutting him off. He'd probably heard that story a million times. Neil checked his watch and sighed, and the cop peered across at Emily. "Get comfortable," he said. "This could take a while."

Neil watched the cop walk back to his car and climb in, and he wondered what curveball could possibly come next.

Thirty-Three

Candy had purchased a sweater at the hotel gift shop, along with a pair of sweatpants. She was still wearing her sandals, the ones she had worn in the hospital after Emily brought them from the ranch. She was exhausted, uncomfortably warm and achy, and she just didn't feel well. Her hair, she knew, was a mess. She'd brushed it in the airport bathroom as best she could before tucking everything she had into the same plastic bag she'd left the hospital with, stuffed with only her shampoo and toothbrush, along with the prescription she had yet to fill for her pain meds.

Her eyes ached from staring at the clock as she waited for another passport to arrive. She'd missed her flight and was furious when she realized Neil had the passports. Hell, he had everything, but at least Stella had come through for her like only a fairy godmother could.

"Candy?"

She heard the familiar voice and jumped around in her seat, wincing from the sharp pain in her stomach at the sudden movement. Then he was in front of her, hovering over her, touching her shoulder, and she didn't have the strength to push him away. He sank down in the empty chair beside her, and she noticed Emily with him.

"What do you want?" she said to Neil. She met his eyes briefly and saw the concern, so she had to look away. No way was she getting sucked back into that after what he'd done. She felt herself choking up and set her trembling fingers to her mouth, struggling to hold it together.

Neil touched her forehead. "Candy, you're clammy and warm. You probably have a fever. Damn them for letting you go. You should still be in the hospital!"

"I'm going home, Neil. Stella has already——"

"There's no passport coming, Candy."

She glanced up at Emily first, who frowned and nodded. Then she narrowed her eyes at Neil. "Stella lied to me?"

"Candy, you need to listen to Neil," Emily interrupted, standing right in front of her.

"Why? He stole my property. It was all he ever wanted, and now he's got it. He didn't have to marry me, and now, since…" She couldn't say the words, that she had lost the baby and had a hysterectomy. Her tongue thickened and wouldn't move.

"Candy, I didn't steal your property. That piece of land was the only thing that always came between us, so I was walking away. The bank took it, and it was gone. I was happy about that because it was you I wanted, but then I found out that a developer was buying it and planning on building condos up and down the beach. I knew you wouldn't be able to live with that, so I bought it. After, I didn't know how to tell you. I was waiting for the right time, which never came."

"So when does the construction start on your fancy resort?" she spat out.

"It doesn't," he said, watching for her reaction.

"I don't understand. You want that resort. You hounded my father for years for that property! You dreamed of that resort…"

"Yes, I did, but I also dreamed of you, Candy. I still want that resort, but I can't just go ahead and build it."

She must have been in worse shape than she thought, because Neil was making no sense. Maybe it was her expression of confusion and puzzlement that made him reply.

"The property is in your name, Candy."

She wasn't sure she had heard him right. "I don't understand. How can it be in my name if you bought it?"

"I bought it for you because you love it," he said, sliding his arm over the back of the seat she was sitting in. He moved closer to her, turning and leaning forward so that she had to look at him.

"But what about your resort?" she asked again.

"Well, that was the reason I was having trouble telling you. I knew you'd believe I had an ulterior motive for the property, which is why it was in your name. I wanted you to trust me enough to know I wouldn't just start building a resort on something you loved so much, but I didn't know how to convince you to let me build it."

"I don't know what to say, Neil," she said.

"There's nothing to say, because I can't build on something that's yours."

When she glanced up at Emily, what she saw was someone she trusted watching Neil with compassion.

"I don't want you to go, Candy," he said. He reached for her hand, and she couldn't see him through the sheen of tears.

"But you didn't want me, and you blame me now because I can't have kids," she said, choking on her tears.

Neil put his other arm around her to block her from other passengers. "Candy, I was furious with you, and I still am. This is about trust, and when I found out you hadn't told me how you were feeling, even after we had just gone through the same thing about the wedding plans, I felt betrayed. I didn't stay because I didn't want to hurt you with what I'd say. I wanted to shake some sense into you, and I wanted to yell at you. That's what I would have done if I'd stayed, but I never would have said I didn't want you. I want children so badly, and you knew that, but I also want you. I was confused because I couldn't separate you from our children. I shouldn't have left you alone. You should have told me of the complications and how you were feeling, because we should share everything, and I should have told you I bought your property."

She didn't understand what he was saying. "Neil, maybe it's too late for us. Maybe there's been too much hurt between us."

"I'm not willing to throw it all away yet, Candy. Are you?" he asked.

She stared at this difficult man and then up at Emily, who encouraged her to answer him. She sighed, not pulling away from the only man to have her whole heart. "No, I guess I'm not, either."

Neil pulled her against him and then whispered, "Let's get you into bed."

He scooped her in his arms and carried her out of the airport, and Candy sighed as she caught the odd looks from strangers. Emily watched her with an expression of support, as if maybe she was beginning to understand her man.

Thirty~Four

Candy brushed her straight, dark hair and applied just a hint of makeup to a complexion that once again had some nice color. She slipped her robe off and stared at her body in the full-length mirror. She wore a lacy white bra and matching underwear, and she ran her finger over the healed scar. It hurt; not physically, but emotionally—the pain of what she couldn't give Neil, the choice taken from her, an ache they now shared. She slipped on a simple white dress, nothing fancy, just knee length and sleeveless.

After a month of lying around and resting, she felt better, but she also felt restless. Both she and Neil had come through a life-altering experience, with a lot of hurtful and harsh words spoken by both of them, but now when he yelled and said what was on his mind, he didn't leave her side, not for one minute. He hugged her and held her.

She remembered the night he had driven them back to Brad's. She'd leaned against his shoulder and slept most of the way. When they pulled in, the family had rallied around her. Diana, Emily, and Becky had made it clear to her that she was one of them now, family, and family didn't run. Two days later, Neil had flown them home, and she'd been recouping ever since. This time, Neil stayed beside her and held her every night while they slept.

Candy stared at the envelope in front of her, the same envelope Neil had given her the first day home. It held the property ownership papers, in her name, for the property Neil had bought for her. Not once since that day had he approached her or asked her about building his resort. The property was hers to do with as she wanted.

He loved her. She loved him. He wanted children, and she saw the emptiness in his gaze every time she looked at him. It would always be a shadow between them, but they talked and mourned together. There were options they still had, and they decided they would explore them together.

A tap on the bedroom door stirred her from her thoughts. Neil stepped in, all fitted in a dark suit and red tie that brought out the bronze in his whiskey-colored eyes.

"Wow, you look gorgeous." He bent down and kissed her. "Are you ready?"

She stared deeply into his eyes and then reached up to touch his smooth jaw. "I am, but first I wanted to give you a wedding present."

He pulled a face and then laughed. "You don't have to give me anything! Besides, wouldn't you rather wait until after we're married?" Neil asked her.

"No. After the ceremony is family time. Besides, I wanted to give you this before," she said, handing him the white envelope.

"What's this?" He hesitated in taking the envelope, sliding out the papers, and reading her handwritten note. "I don't understand."

"It's self-explanatory. I'm giving you the property to

build your resort," she said, watching as his expression softened. "I trust you, Neil, and I know how much that resort means to you. I just have one request."

"Only one?" He pulled her into his arms and hugged her so tight. He kissed her deeply, sliding both hands over her cheeks and pulling back just enough to watch her.

She licked her lips, still tasting him. "I want a part of the beach to remain private for me. I'd like to have a private place to ride Sable that's not flooded with people, a place that's just ours, a place that only you and I can go."

Neil tucked her long hair behind her ears. It was a good thing she hadn't primped for hours or cared that her hair and makeup were pristine. "I'll tell you what; you'll have that piece for you, for us, but you'll also know every detail of the resort. No secrets."

"No secrets," she whispered back.

Neil tucked the papers into his jacket pocket and then took her hand. "Are you ready?"

"I am more than ready to be your wife," she said.

Neil walked her outside. There was no band, no musicians, just their garden, a few flowers, and Neil's parents, along with Emily and Brad, and Jed and Diana, standing with them. Francesco, a short, dark-haired Mayan wearing a simple white shirt and dark pants, would marry them.

All of the kids were there, as was their friend, Stella, decked out in a red cocktail dress and heels that had all the men taking a second look. Andy and Laura, sadly, were on their way to Montana and hadn't been able to come. Neil had been disappointed, but he'd promised Andy they'd come and visit once he and Laura got settled.

The wedding was short, simple, and had been planned entirely by Candy after she'd told Neil, in no uncertain terms, that there was no way he would plan any part of it —Becky had stood beside her when she told him.

The ceremony was quick and simple, and the ring Neil placed on Candy's finger was made of six large diamonds surrounding a beautiful, square, pink one. As Candy stood in Neil's arms, with his family around them, she knew without any doubt that she was now a Friessen.

The Friessens are returning!

Turn the page for a sneak peek of
*The Deadline the return of the Friessen family in The Friessens: A
New Beginning*
Available in print, audio & eBook.

—"Author Lorhainne Eckhart is adept at showing deeply felt emotions through actions, instead of just telling us. The insecurity, fear and paranoia practically emanated from Laura at the beginning of the story and watching her find her strength was truly an honor." ~ Reviewed by Natasha Jackson, Readers Favorite

—"This book will steal your heart & have you waiting for the next one. It will also teach you to speak your mind when necessary. I do hope this situation never happens in real life! Don't miss a very good emotional read." - Whodunnit, Reviewer

—"I love these Friessen men and their families. Was so excited the stories are going to keep on how going. Andy and Laura had a plate full with a sick child and moving to a new state along with twins. Andy has a strong personality and I appreciate him more after this book. What a man won't do for his family. Please read!" - Janet Murphy, Reviewer

—"I'm like your other fans, absolutely in love with this family. I so wanted Gabriel to get well and can't wait until Andy's mother finally gets what's coming to her. I've never read of such a vicious, manipulative, heartless character like her before. I love how this family comes together for each *other, and the hubbies, momma mia, so masterful, hunks personified. I personally could see this as a series on TV." - Arkansan, Reviewer*

—"I loved this book! Thank You Lorhainne Eckhart for bringing the Friessens back. You make the Friessen men so alive and the kind of men us women wish we could meet. The Deadline is a touching story of unconditional love and strength." - Amazon Customer, Reviewer

In **THE DEADLINE**, Andy Friessen has packed up everything and moved his family two states away, to Montana, to protect his wife, Laura, his newborn babies, and his stepson, Gabriel, from the threats of his mother. What Andy doesn't know is that they'll soon face a new threat, one he never saw coming.

Gabriel is sick, and a trip to the doctor confirms Laura and Andy's worst nightmare: Without a lifesaving transplant, their son won't survive.

What Andy doesn't count on, as he tracks down the young man who fathered Gabriel, as well as Laura's estranged parents, is that a whole host of problems are about to be unleashed.

Chapter 1

How do you describe the feeling you get the first time you drive down a long, winding road to a place that is all yours? To Andy Friessen, this wasn't just a house or a piece of land: he had staked a claim in another state, in another part of the country, uprooting his family and selling everything, all for a brand new beginning.

Andy took in the miles of vast hillside and the cleanest pastures he'd ever seen. The green grass swayed in the wind and, for the first time, he sensed the sun, the moon, the stars and the changing of the seasons more deeply than he ever had before. This was a part of the country he had never travelled, but it felt like coming home. He glanced over at his wife, Laura, asleep in the passenger seat, her head resting against the door, her breath whispering softly in and out. He always knew when she was overtired, as she snored in her soft, delicate way. This time, she stirred a bit before settling into a deep sleep, as if her body had finally run out of steam.

She was on edge and had been for some time, but that

wasn't unusual for a mother of newborns. For Andy and Laura, there was twice as much stress with their six-week-old twins, Chelsea and Jeremy, who were sound asleep in the backseat of the truck. Their five-year-old big brother, Gabriel, Laura's son from a pregnancy at fifteen, sat beside them.

Laura was so young but had lived through more heartache, rejection and struggle than most people would in a lifetime. As a teenager, she had been tossed out onto the street by her judgmental parents, who thought she was a bad influence on her younger brothers. Laura had only mentioned it once to Andy, and only when he pushed. He wanted to know what had happened, to know everything about her family, but he saw the deep hurt like a tread mark on her soul. No matter what he did, he wondered if that was something she'd never be able to make peace with. Andy wouldn't, not in this lifetime. In fact, George and Sue Parnell were the first people Andy had ever hated without even meeting them.

They had come so far, Laura and him. At first, the only reason he had married her was to save her son when the state took him away. Laura and Gabriel had been living in her car, and Andy had married her because he felt responsible for the entire mess. After all, it had been his mother who fired Laura from her position as a maid in the Friessen house. Andy had treated her horribly at first, but so much had changed since then. He loved her—his child bride, as everyone teased him. She had recently turned twenty-one, legal in every state, and Andy would soon be thirty-three.

Andy pressed the brakes to slow his pickup as the ruts deepened on the driveway. The horse trailer rattled, and he glanced in the side mirror and rolled down his window just as his three-year-old buckskin mare, Ladystar, nickered. Apparently, she'd had enough of this two-day trip, leaving North Lakewood behind and moving two states away to a seventy-two-acre spread Andy had purchased outside of Columbia Falls, Montana.

"Where are we?" Laura said. She didn't open her eyes as she yawned. Her short bob was a tangled mess, but it was cute. Andy had been irritated when she cut off all her hair, saying it was easier to look after. Maybe so, but he liked her long hair. "Andy?" she said. The leather seat rustled as she sat up.

Andy had to clear his throat. "We should be close. ..."

He stepped on the brakes when a sprawling one-story ranch house came into view. It had a light wood finish and a post-and-beam front deck, but something about the place didn't look right. The railing appeared broken, with pieces of wood scattered here and there. Everything looked unkempt. Piles of debris littered the yard, including a rusted-out pickup with missing wheels parked in waist-high grass that was now weighted down by the melting snow. Maybe he had the wrong place? He eased on the gas pedal and started up the slight incline that circled the house. It was similar to the photos he had seen, but the house in the photos had been newer than this. A couple of the shutters were hanging sideways, and the fence surrounding the house was falling down, as was the corral, but it was the junk, the debris, the plastic, garbage and scattered metal parts, that pissed him off.

"What the hell is this?"

He'd bought the place unseen. The Montana realtor had sent photos of the exterior and interior, and maybe Andy should have asked when they had been taken, but he'd been in a hurry to get Laura and the kids as far away from his family as he could. He parked in front of the house and spotted the red and white realty sign leaning against the front step.

"Andy, this doesn't look like the pictures the realtor sent," Laura said. "Are you sure this is the right place?"

One of the babies started fussing, and Ladystar nickered from the trailer.

"Andy, are we here?" Gabriel called out from the backseat, rubbing his eyes.

"Yeah, just stay there, bud," Andy said as he opened his door. Laura was reaching over to unbuckle Jeremy from his car seat, his tiny hands flailing. "He hungry?"

Laura appeared so tired as she nodded. "I think so. Wet, too." She patted his bottom and rested him on the seat. "Andy, can you reach the diaper bag on the floor in the back?" She had already unfastened his sleeper as Andy lifted the blue bag, shut the back door and set the bag on his seat.

"Just stay in here until I check things out," he said.

Laura glanced up with a weary smile. "Okay."

He shut the door and stepped around the truck, taking in the mess. Ladystar nickered again. "Okay, girl," he murmured, unlatching the horse trailer and leading his horse out before tying her to the side and bringing out a flake of hay for her. "Better find you some water, too," he said, pulling out his bucket. Around the side of the house, he found a barn with a missing door, another gated pasture, and a round ring. As he stepped closer, he noticed the round pen appeared intact, with no missing posts and all the rails up. It was probably a safe bet for tonight, at least for Ladystar, until he got a better look around.

He found a water tap at the back of the house and turned it on, but rusty water poured out. "Crap!" he muttered, waiting for it to run clear before he filled the bucket. When he took it back to the trailer where Ladystar was tied and eating, Laura opened the door of the truck and called out, "Andy, Gabriel has to go to the bathroom, and so do I. Can we go inside?"

Andy took in what was supposed to have been a ten-year-old sprawling rancher, with a wraparound deck where they could spend evenings and mornings looking out over their spread. Instead, it resembled the kind of house his cousin Jed would have picked up for a good price to gut and renovate—not something Andy was interested in doing.

"All right," Andy said. He opened the back door and lifted Gabriel, who was already unbuckled and waiting. "Stay here, Gabriel. Hey, Laura, Chelsea is still sleeping." Andy lifted his very quiet daughter from the car.

Laura slid down, carrying Jeremy, who was fussing again. She had on just a beige sweater. "Ooh, it's cold," she said. She reached in the truck for her jacket and pulled it out, holding it out to Andy so he could help her as she juggled the baby.

Laura started up the steps, and Gabriel and Andy followed. At the sound of a vehicle coming down the road, they both turned to see a newer pickup truck flying over the ruts and then pulling in just behind the horse trailer. A woman with a round face, bright smile, and dark hair tied back in a ponytail stepped out, wearing a sheepskin coat and blue jeans.

Laura shrieked behind Andy. He turned just as the screen door Laura had pulled fell over and crashed to the front deck. Chelsea, who had been sleeping, whimpered and then started howling along with her brother.

"Lorhainne Eckhart is one of my go to authors when I want a guaranteed good book. So many twists and turns, but also so much love and such a strong sense of family."

(LORA W., REVIEWER)

New York Times & USA Today bestseller Lorhainne Eckhart is best known for writing Raw Relatable Real Romance where "Morals and family are running themes." As one fan calls her, she is the "Queen of the family saga." (aherman) writing "the ups and downs of what goes on within a family but also with some suspense, angst and of course a bit of romance thrown in for good measure."

Follow Lorhainne on Bookbub to receive alerts on New Releases and Sales and join her mailing list at Lorhainne-Eckhart.com for her Monday Blog, all book news, give-aways and FREE reads. With over 120 books, audiobooks, and multiple series published and available at all, retailers now translated into six languages. She is a multiple recipient of the Readers' Favorite Award for Suspense and Romance, and lives in the Pacific Northwest on an island, is the mother of three, her oldest has autism and she is an advocate for never giving up on your dreams.

"Lorhainne Eckhart has this uncanny way of just hitting the spot every time with her books."

(CAROLINE L., REVIEWER)

The O'Connells: *The O'Connells of Livingston, Montana are not your typical family. A riveting collection of stories surrounding the ups and downs of what goes on within a family but also with some suspense, angst and of course a bit of romance thrown in for good measure. "I thought I loved the Friessens, but I absolutely adore the O'Connell's. Each and every book has different genres of stories, but the one thing in common is how she is able to wrap it around the family, which is the heart of each story." (C. Logue)*

The Friessens: *An emotional big family romance series, the Friessen family siblings find their relationships tested, lay their hearts on the line, and discover lasting love! "Lorhainne Eckhart is one of my go to authors when I want* *a guaranteed good book. So many twists and turns, but also so much love and such a strong sense of family." (Lora W., Reviewer)*

The Parker Sisters: *The Parker Sisters are a close-knit family, and like any other family they have their ups and downs. Eckhart has crafted another intense family drama… "The character development is outstanding, and the emotional investment is high…" (Aherman, Reviewer)*

The McCabe Brothers: *Join the five McCabe siblings on their journeys to the dark and dangerous side of love! An intense, exhilarating collection of romantic thrillers you won't want to miss. — "Eckhart has a new series that is definitely worth the read. The queen of the family saga started this series with a spin-off of her wildly successful Friessen series." From a Readers' Favorite award—winning author and "queen of the family saga" (Aherman)*

Lorhainne loves to hear from her readers! You can connect with me at:
www.LorhainneEckhart.com
lorhainneeckhart.le@gmail.com

The Outsider Series

The Forgotten Child (Brad and Emily)
A Baby and a Wedding *(An Outsider Series Short)*
Fallen Hero (Andy, Jed, and Diana)
The Search *(An Outsider Series Short)*
The Awakening (Andy and Laura)
Secrets (Jed and Diana)
Runaway (Andy and Laura)
Overdue *(An Outsider Series Short)*
The Unexpected Storm (Neil and Candy)
The Wedding (Neil and Candy)

The Friessens: A New Beginning

The Deadline (Andy and Laura)
The Price to Love (Neil and Candy)
A Different Kind of Love (Brad and Emily)
A Vow of Love, A Friessen Family Christmas

The Friessens

The Reunion
The Bloodline (Andy & Laura)
The Promise (Diana & Jed)
The Business Plan (Neil & Candy)
The Decision (Brad & Emily)
First Love (Katy)
Family First
Leave the Light On
In the Moment
In the Family

In the Silence
In the Charm
Unexpected Consequences
It Was Always You
The First Time I Saw You
Welcome to My Arms
Welcome to Boston
I'll Always Love You
Ground Rules
A Reason to Breathe
You Are My Everything
Anything For You
The Homecoming
Stay Away From My Daughter
The Bad Boy
A Place of Our Own
The Visitor
All About Devon
Long Past Dawn
How to Heal a Heart
Keep Me In Your Heart

The O'Connells
The Neighbor
The Third Call
The Secret Husband
The Quiet Day
The Commitment
The Missing Father
The Hometown Hero
Justice
The Family Secret
The Fallen O'Connell
The Return of the O'Connells

And The She Was Gone
The Stalker
The O'Connell Family Christmas
The Girl Next Door
Broken Promises
The Gatekeeper
The Hunted

The McCabe Brothers
Don't Stop Me (Vic)
Don't Catch Me (Chase)
Don't Run From Me (Aaron)
Don't Hide From Me (Luc)
Don't Leave Me (Claudia)
Out of Time

A Billy Jo McCabe Mystery
Nothing As it Seems
Hiding in Plain Sight
The Cold Case
The Trap
Above the Law
The Stranger at the Door
The Children
The Last Stand
The Charity
The Sacrifice

The Street Fighter
Finding Home

The Wilde Brothers
The One (Joe and Margaret)
The Honeymoon, A Wilde Brothers Short

Friendly Fire (Logan and Julia)
Not Quite Married, A Wilde Brothers Short
A Matter of Trust (Ben and Carrie)
The Reckoning, A Wilde Brothers Christmas
Traded (Jake)
Unforgiven (Samuel)
The Holiday Bride

Married in Montana
His Promise
Love's Promise
A Promise of Forever

The Parker Sisters
Thrill of the Chase
The Dating Game
Play Hard to Get
What We Can't Have
Go Your Own Way
A June Wedding

Kate & Walker
One Night
Edge of Night
Last Night

Walk the Right Road Series
The Choice
Lost and Found
Merkaba
Bounty
Blown Away: The Final Chapter
He Came Back

The Saved Series
Saved
Vanished
Captured

Single Titles
Loving Christine